The Cognitive Web

by Eldon Cene

ISBN:0692722831
ISBN-13:9780692722831

DEDICATION

To all my summertime readers relaxing in a gentle breeze surrounded by the sloshing of the surf, the chirping of tropical birds and the laughter of happy children. I'm in a damn prison cell, you know.

Look for all these books on the Magic Bean label.

Magic Bean Books

Plays by Carl Nelson:
Into the Wild Blue Yonder
Personal Growth Through Copier Sales
Ollie's Day Out

Essays by Carl Nelson:
The Audience is a Mob
The Pyramid of Rational Thought and How It Leads to Extinction

Poetry by Carl Nelson:
A Poet's Past Lives
Shoving My Way Into the Conversation
I'm Forgetting Things in My Dreams

Fiction by Eldon Cene
Murders In Progress
The Cognitive Web
The Mind Wars

All are currently available through Amazon books.

http://www.magicbeanbooks.co/home.html

CONTENTS

ACKNOWLEDGMENTS

I'm sure Eldon would be quick to agree that extreme thanks be paid to our publisher, Magic Bean Books, for taking on what has turned out to be quite an undertaking - to resurrect this manuscript from blemished and torn copy and scraps of notes and letters left by Eldon himself. As estate executor I'm also responsible and take full responsibility for the addendums and inclusions and bridges of prose which have eventually pulled the entire trilogy together. The fallout of its publication, both politically and artistically, is something that is to be seen.

- Carl Nelson

Editor's Introduction to *The Cognitive Web*

"All fiction is crime fiction." - Eldon Cene

I

When I told our dear readers of Eldon Cene's death, in part I misspoke. Eldon, actually, is *presumed* dead. Though taking into account what his current age would be, it would be quite surprising if Eldon were still alive. In actuality, we have no evidence of Eldon's death. It is all circumstantial. What Eldon actually did was to 'disappear'.

Now it might sound strange to disappear from a federal prison like Lumpoc. But it is not unknown. Previous to Eldon's disappearance have been several other prisoner disappearances that have been thoroughly investigated and reported. No further evidence has come to light since those times, and so those prisoners, like Eldon, have bureaucratically been characterized as deceased. Whether they *are* or not we may never know. Certainly there is no record or indication of their escape. No one on the outside has confessed to seeing any of these vanished prisoners. And neither has anyone on the inside (excepting for the habitual nutcases) remarked on seeing them reappear. One day they were here. The next day they were gone. In some cases a dribble of blood, in other cases a smattering of what was taken to be hairs and skull fragments remained.

Where the bodies might be, no one knows. Some insist that Lompoc was built over preexisting structures whose hidden passageways and unknown dungeons are still contained within its rock walls but sealed over. Others believe that Eldon most probably killed these prisoners and then minced them up to be served in a spicy chili or beef burgeon to the other prisoners at their next meal. (Eldon was a cook at the prison.) Or perhaps they were just flushed. How he managed this is the source of a lot more conjecture.

But most of the prisoners believe that, save Eldon, the missing convicts were murdered. They don't know how but, in several cases, they contend they know why: "They disrespected Eldon." Or they 'took on' Eldon. It's simple as that many feel. As for Eldon himself, many prisoners believe he took himself off to wherever the other prisoners went. Maybe he got away; maybe not.

I, myself, must report that when I visited Eldon in his latter years at Lumpoc Correctional Institution, he seemed to be accorded enormous respect. Other convicts remained at least a yard from him at all times, even in passing, holding him in what appeared to be awe. Even the largest, most brutal appearing convict would pause, allowing Eldon to pass through a doorway first.

I asked Eldon about this during one of my interview/visits. And he reported that it wasn't always so, but was something which had gradually just come about. I said that was 'nice'. He smiled slightly and agreed. Eldon appeared to be the sort who was of no threat to anyone as long as he was left alone to write. He certainly didn't display any need to project his power. He came and went. He obeyed the guards. When others spoke, he replied. And when he spoke, others replied. He didn't demand his channel in the TV room. He didn't cut to the head of the line in the lunch room. He shared the phone. (He rarely used it.) He didn't care if others held his opinions. "He was a great guy, really. You just didn't fuck with him." This latter seemed to be what was generally agreed - at least in the prison ghost stories told to many of the newbies.

When we were talking one time about the murders in his many books, Eldon noted that the best way to murder anyone - and that this would be especially true in a prison - would be to just make them disappear. "When a person disappears," Eldon said, "there's nothing. No evidence. No time of commission. No one knows how they disappeared. No one knows *why* they disappeared. In fact, no one knows even *if* they've disappeared. They are just not there. This gives the murderer a tremendous advantage. There are no clues; or perhaps everything is a clue. There is no forewarning; or perhaps we can't recognize one. There is no knowledge about the crime of any sort. All of which conjures up the most menacing and diabolical fantasies in the minds of the survivors. Since they don't know how the deceased became deceased, they don't have any way of knowing how to prevent the same thing happening to themselves. Which means, at least in a prison environment, that they are very respectful to the person or persons who they most think might have done it. Whatever *it* was." He smiled.

This was all Eldon said about it, and the only time he broached the topic. To be sure, I was very respectful of Eldon myself.

II

While Eldon acknowledged the necessity of accurate factual detail in fabricating a captivating read, he disliked regurgitated knowledge, regarding it as the "purview of blowhards. Jerks, who someone has taught to read, all good sense notwithstanding. Who then sally forth to spread their imbecility with a trowel, as if with a notary's stamp upon it."

One thing Eldon loved about criminal enterprise was its confidentiality. "When I uncover a fact here in Lompoc, it's like the freshest fish pulled right out of the sea and served up on a platter with a little dill, lemon juice and butter. It doesn't have the bookish stink of the library or that awful putrid aura of some long ago publication hovering over it. It's like the difference between virtual sex and the real smelly stuff," he added. (Though he acknowledged dryly, that he was operating on "deep memory" there.)

Eldon was constantly talking to his fellow prisoners, rarely asking questions ("Every question is a 'leading' question", he was fond of saying.) but seemingly just passing the time. "I'm in no rush," he repeated often. Though why he would have to be in a rush, or exactly what he was trying to accomplish, I couldn't say for a fact, other than the fact that he *was* a writer. But, in truth, in spite of what he said, his last few months seemed to have been very rushed, indeed. In his last interviews with me his words came in bursts; his eyes were wont to dart to the side, and his epithets were laced with what would sound to be governmental acronyms whenever he found the need to hiss into a bag. (He had emphysema.)

Eldon said he had spoken with innumerable interesting people there in Lumpoc, but that the latest prisoner who had happened upon his block was in a "whole, different league." "I don't know why he's here. Or what it is that made the powers that be think that this would be an appropriate place for him. His presence here would seem to put them at great risk." He spoke in a low, hoarse voice. "I don't know why they've left him alive, to tell the truth," he added. "But I hope to get to the bottom of it. This tale could put me on the map." He had smiled enigmatically. After 31 unpublished novels, I figured he figured he finally had a saleable property. And no matter what Eldon said, I know that every author yearns for audience.

Well, he hasn't quite made it. This last known manuscript of Eldon's wasn't found until months after his disappearance. The next inmate to inherit his cell had tried to destroy everything in it after going crazy following drinking some bad prison hooch. In the course of flushing the mattress stuffing down the toilet, his 'craziness' pulled out a stained manuscript of Eldon's, titled, *The Cognitive Web*. Which the prisoner, oddly enough, stopped to read. This is the manuscript of the story you are about to read here, excepting for some written additions and adjustments made by myself for reasons of story coherence, since some portions of the manuscript were lost, and others obliterated by stains (some of them brown, and some of it - flushed). I believe, however, that I have gotten Eldon's final novel as near to the truth of what he had intended to be passed on as is possible.

A number of questions still haunt us though. He was a mild man of slight build, imprisoned in a ferocious place. How did Eldon command his reputation? How did he make his enemies disappear? Who was Prisoner #3915? (This is the pseudonym Eldon used in his note taking.) And whatever happened to Eldon, himself? Why did Eldon hide a final manuscript in his mattress? Was there governmental involvement? And of what sort, and how high up might it have gone? And has it all blown over and 'died' with Eldon and the disappearance of Prisoner #3915, or are the events fictionalized in this found manuscript still in play today?

Perhaps, in my conversations with Eldon, he left us with a few clues...

But maybe I won't tell you those. Let's see if you can glean them from the story which follows.

- Carl Nelson May, 2016

The Cognitive Web

Colin Mayfield

Colin Mayfield, age 15, loved Nancy Gillis. He planned to marry her, and being a straightforward boy told her as much.

"I'm not ready for marriage Colin," Nancy told him in no uncertain terms. "We're only 15."

"Lots of kids are only 15, and they're already *pregnant* Nancy," Colin urged.

"You want to get me *pregnant?*"

"No!" Colin exclaimed. "I'm just saying that kids, everywhere, are... getting on with their lives. And that maybe we should too?"

"I am getting on with my life, Colin." Nancy looked up from the computer from where she was working. "I'm well on my way to becoming a world class reporter."

"That's great! I admire that about you Nancy," Colin replied earnestly. "I love a strong woman. And I'm not saying that we have to go right out and tie the knot, today."

Nancy breathed a mock sigh of relief.

"I'm just talking, okay? I'm just letting you know how I feel, that's all. I mean, after all, people who are 15 don't get married. I know that."

"I wonder." Nancy pecked at a letter.

"They might get *pregnant*. But that's not what I'm looking for either."

"That's great. Since we haven't even *kissed*." Nancy pecked out two more letters.

"I just thought that I'd mention it now. You know. Many years before the actual act. So that you don't feel pressured."

"Trust me." Nancy stared at Colin coldly. "I don't feel *pressured*."

Colin sometimes had a hard time knowing how Nancy felt about him. Most people liked Colin, but Nancy Gillis wasn't *most* people. Nancy Gillis was like a fast moving fire, Colin would say many years later when he mulled his past. He didn't know why. He doubted she knew why. He just knew that she was the most determined girl he had ever met. She got her teeth into something, and she didn't let go. It was almost scary. Colin had the inclination to think that it was probably much better - or at least safer - that he loved her more than she appeared to love him. But he didn't drink at that time, 15 year olds being more action oriented than reflective. And so he spent his waking hours trying to figure how to gain her attention.

He remembered his father's words: "Well Colin, women are a lot like anything else. If you're around it a lot, you'll probably end up with it." And so he followed his father's words. (Not realizing at the time that diseases are like that.) But he didn't know whether it was helping or not. Which made him recall another of his father's sayings, "We take the advice we like." And in this respect, his father's advice had seemed *great*. So Colin just kept on doing what he was doing. And it wasn't like there was a long line of people just waiting to talk to Nancy.

Colin had a good mind to tell her that; that he was probably the only friend she had! But that probably wasn't going to get him into her good graces either. So Colin pedaled around town following her everywhere.

"If you don't watch it, I might write about you," Nancy said one day, looking up from her keyboard. "My Experience with a Stalker" by Nancy Gillis", Nancy spread her hands to indicate the banner headline above her head. "In the New York Times, a *National* newspaper."

"And you could do it too!" Colin said admiringly.

Nancy sighed, shook her head, and then went back to work.

However, over the next few months, Colin followed Nancy a little more *clandestinely* - which was another word he had picked up from speaking with Nancy. And he got to become pretty good at just 'bumping into' her, 'here and there'. 'Bumping into her' later on at the Sheriff's office was a little more difficult, but Colin put his mind to it. He would walk in and ask Ruth what their lunch and dinner preferences for that day might be. And then, after finding Nancy there and hanging around quite a while - he would take these written dinner preferences over to Carmella, who had never asked for them in the first place. Both Ruth and Carmella thought he was running errands for the other.

Nancy though called him on it, but before he could say anything added, "You're a lot more resourceful than I'd have thought."

When she nodded, Colin thought he might have detected her estimation of him climbing just a wee bit. Which did wonders to spur Colin on. Very few people could keep track of Nancy, but Colin would.

So when Nancy disappeared that Monday morning into the Sheriff's Jeep and went squealing away with Ruth at the wheel and the siren blaring and the lights flashing - Colin was there to track her down. The Sheriff's vehicle itself soon outdistanced him. But Colin had pedaled hard enough and fast enough to note which route the Sheriff's vehicle had taken out of town. It was heading north. And when Colin stopped and stood real still, he could still hear the faint bleating of the siren several minutes away. So, from experience Colin figured they were headed somewhere to the north at least 3 miles off. Ramey, the dentist, lived out that way. And what made Colin think of that was the fact that the woman who'd gotten into the back had looked a lot like Ramey the dentist. It probably wasn't, he told himself. It couldn't be. Nevertheless, he reasoned, it gave him somewhere to go and some place to check out. It would be quite a peddle. But that was just one of the things you do for love.

Nancy Gillis Opens the Door

"For goodness sakes! What the heck do *you* want?" Nancy asked, after answering the dentist Ramey's door and seeing a sweating, exhausted Colin standing there.

This wasn't quite the reception Colin was seeking. But finding her was really all the reward he needed. "It's you! You're here!" He cried.

"Of course I'm here," Nancy snapped. "Now get inside and quit shouting," she ordered. "This home is supposed to be vacated," she hissed, pulling Colin inside and shutting the door. "Wait!" She shoved him back outside again. "Go hide your bike… out in the shed where the Sheriff's vehicle is parked." Colin was about to do this, when she hissed and pulled at him again. "Wait! Do you have a cell phone?" Colin nodded, starting to dig it out of his pocket, when Nancy shoved him off. "No, no. That wouldn't matter. No one knows that you're even connected."

Colin didn't know what to make of this. But he went and hid his bike and then followed where Nancy led him down a hall into the daylight basement with all the blinds shut. As his eyes adjusted, Colin noted many other people there.

"I might as well introduce you around," Nancy said. "That fellow over there is our prisoner. So give him a wide berth."

"Hi, Stan… former Special Forces/ Black Op/ Marriage Therapist/ Short Order Cook/and Serial Killer just recovering from a cheap blow to the head from an unwitting third party." Stan glowered at Ramey.

Stan nodded at Colin. "You want to be my friend?"

Colin opened his mouth, but no words appeared.

"And you remember Ruth."

Ruth nodded.

Colin nodded.

"And Dr. Ramey."

Colin's brows collected as Dr. Ramey looked embarrassed.

"Dr. Ramey is currently in the possession of a rather violent spirit - of the female gender," Nancy added. "Goes by the name of Nancy Loomis, alias the Muffin Lady."

"We're sharing the space, actually," the Muffin Lady replied.

Colin nodded his head, clearly bewildered.

"And then there's me, and Agent Hailey."

Colin had seen Agent Hailey around. He nodded.

"Do you have a cell phone?" Agent Hailey asked.

"Yes," Colin replied.

"Would you mind if I borrowed it?"

Colin gave it to her.

"Thanks." Agent Hailey smiled and began making some calls.

"Golly, I'm sure glad to see you're okay Nancy," Colin blurted once they were off by themselves.

"I'm fine," Nancy stated, pulling him further aside. "Now what are you doing out here?"

"Finding out if you're okay!" Colin said. "And if I could be of help," he added. "After all, the whole Sheriff's office blew sky high. A van load of Japanese tourists were washtubbed. And you went racing off with several people I hardly know in the Sheriff's SUV."

"You've been spying on me!"

"Well. You spy on everybody else."

"Yeah. But I'm a professional. And it isn't spying, it's *reporting*. It's not spying if your end is to publish the information publicly, and you have the widespread credibility to do so."

"I didn't think you'd want what I know reported publicly."

"Well," Nancy considered. "You're right there. Still. That *does* make it spying."

"Okay. Fine. I'm sorry."

Nancy thought a bit. "Apology accepted," she said finally. "And maybe there *is* something you can do for me."

"Sure." Colin smiled. "Will it help me gain *credibility*?"

6

"I think so," Nancy replied.

"Then I'm in," Colin stated.

"Now you need to impress it upon them very strongly that what they are undertaking could be dangerous - if they let on in any way, and to anyone the thrust of the research they are doing? You got that?" Nancy addressed Colin very seriously.

"Yes," Colin answered.

Nancy liked one word answers. I meant whoever said it was doing nothing but listen. It demonstrated obedience.

"I'm to say I'm doing some kind of a report on West Virginia. And to utilize the school's database to locate several fellow student reporters in the vicinity of Pinch, West Virginia. I Skype interview them in order to gauge which might be the most trustworthy and useful student. And then I offer this one a byline in the New York Times if he - or *she* - can get us a list of names and other identifying information of the people who were on the School Bus which 'disappeared' for 6 hours while heading to Charleston on October 23rd, 1986. Once obtaining these, they are to research everything about the current situations and whereabouts of these people. And also to research any other leads of interest that my come up during said investigation." Colin took a deep breath.

"I am to repeat," Colin continued, "the importance of highest security in carrying out this investigation and to suggest cloaking the whole endeavor under the work around of some other newsworthy event occurring around this date and time. They are *not* to trust the state, local or federal governments, or other reporters. And using an alias or several, at critical junctures during your research, might be prudent. Also using a variety of publicly accessed computer terminals would be advised. And keep your access brief."

"Oh! And *don't delay*. Delay only gives the advantage to our adversaries, whoever they might be. And any good story is a perishable commodity. We need this information yesterday!" Colin remembered to emphasize.

"Good. Very good," Nancy complimented him. "Now, off with you!" She exclaimed and opened the door, as if releasing a carrier pigeon.

Colin paused in the doorway.

"Oh alright!" Nancy gave Colin a peck on the cheek, and he ran off with a big smile on his face.

"What?" Nancy, turning, asked the others.

Agent Perez

"Where are my people?" Leland demanded.

"Right now, we still don't know."

"Who have you got out there looking?" Leland demanded.

"Just about everybody," Agent Perez said somewhat cryptically. "We've pulled in assets from all the neighboring states. We've got choppers, dogs…"

"Assets, huh." Leland looked the man over skeptically. The man had phoned. Leland had invited him over after speaking with him for 15 seconds. Then Leland had looked up and there he was, complete with an ear bud, walking in the doorway with is hand outstretched.

Leland sighed. "Alright," he said. "So what *do* you know? What have you got?"

Agent Perez, took this as an invitation to sit down.

"From what we know, so far, the explosion was caused by a large collection of propane ignited by a simple device created from tape, likely a balloon, surgical tubing, common table matches, and using the pressure of the propane bottles as the driving force to create a crude but effective timing device," he said. "Certain Special Ops agents are taught how to fashion these devices and many other such things from common materials close at hand. And this device seems to fit that pattern." Agent Perez tossed some glossies taken of evidence onto Leland's desktop.

Leland nodded. A couple days had passed since the blast. And he was just now beginning to feel his head clear and the ringing in his ears stop so that he could follow a normal conversation. Agent Perez looked at him more closely as Leland shuffled through the glossies with the eraser of his pencil.

"I follow," Leland assured him. "What you are saying is that we had unwittingly invited our perp over to the jail to serve us breakfast that morning. A man who intended to blow us all to Kingdom come, but unwittingly got caught in a trap of his own making."

"That's right. Or at least that's our best guess." Agent Perez nodded. "He's of a sort who are used to cutting things close, and he probably was looking forward to 'breaking bread' with you - just before he "blew you all to Kingdom come", as they say."

"And you are sure this is our man, because?" Leland asked.

"Because of all the forensics you sent us," Agent Perez answered.

"We didn't send them to *you*," Leland growled.

"When it's a matter of National Security everything goes through us." Agent Perez' eyes fixed on Leland.

Leland let him know with a glance that this was not pleasing to him. "Which brings to mind a question: Why is this situation a matter of "National Security"? Bad as it is, so far all that has happened is that a couple women have lost their heads. How does a couple women losing their heads imperil National Security?"

Agent Perez laughed slightly.

"It's not the women," Agent Perez responded, flipping a photograph forward. "It's the man."

Leland responded by looking at the photo. It was "Stan" alright. Several years younger and with a tighter haircut, but "Stan" nevertheless.

"I don't know," Leland said. "It could have been him. But like I've said, my memories of the event are pretty checkered. You want my memories of a couple weeks before, and I can give you all the help you need. But that blast seems to have cleared my head pretty good."

"As you probably know that's not uncommon with a brain concussion. In time your memories of the event may come back to you."

Leland nodded. He was sure that this was true.

"But in the meantime, if anything does come back to you, we would appreciate you letting us know."

Leland nodded again.

"What we believe to have happened is that your killer was

working as a cook at the restaurant across the way, while he was for some reason plotting to blow you up. As I've said, he's unhinged, so any answer could be the answer. But it might very well be because of your having shot and killed the farmers hereabout who formerly harbored him, he bore a grudge."

Leland shook his head.

"I'm not saying," Agent Perez spoke with his palms down, "that it wasn't justified or that our killer is in anyway particularly loyal or forms connections with other people easily or at all. But he may have thought of Harriet and Bob Weeds as his 'troops'. That is, when you killed them it was a 'territorial thing'. Good soldiers don't give up ground."

"He's a "good soldier"?"

"*Was*," Agent Perez emphasized. "One of our best. Which is why it is our job to get him back. Not only is he highly trained and especially dangerous, but he is one of ours who had an affinity for eccentric behavior even before a Section 8 discharge. God knows, there are enough of them - that is 'reasons' for going off the deep end - in our line of work. But it isn't the job of local law enforcement jurisdictions to handle these sorts of things. And that was why we impounded all of your information. It was to protect you, and perhaps others."

"That didn't work very well, did it?" Leland said.

"In this case, I'd agree." Agent Perez nodded.

Leland looked Agent Perez over. He wanted to get as good a visual memory of this man as was humanly possible. And then he wanted to get a copy of his ID, too.

"You mind if I make a copy of your ID for our records?" Leland asked. "I'm expecting a meeting with our mayor anytime now and with information as startling as this, a few facts and documentation can really help smooth the path."

Agent Perez shook his head, but nodded, and handed it over.

"Great. And a place and phone number where we can reach you?"

"Certainly." He scrawled this across a notepad and tore it off. "Plus my Twitter and email account." He smiled.

Leland shook his head. "Never tweeted the NSA before."

"We're just like anyone else," Agent Perez said.

"I'll bet you are," Leland said.

After Agent Perez left, Leland sat and watched the afternoon sunlight cut its swath across the cottage floorboards. The town was especially still and quiet in the midday summer sun. In the distance it sounded as though a couple kids were playing in a yard sprinkler. Looking out the cottage door it felt like being in summer camp.

Leland phoned a former college in LA. "Buenos dios, Pablo. Yeah, it's 'farmer' Leland. Hey, look. I'm in a bit of a jam up here." Pause. Leland laughed. "No. I haven't locked myself in my own jail. Actually they blew up my jail." Long pause. "I know, it's unfortunate. But what I would like you to do for *me* is to look up this fellow I'll be faxing to you, to see if he's on the up and up." Leland paused. "Did *he* blow up my jail? I don't' know. Does the government blow up jails?" Leland nodded. "And anything more about him you might be able to find out. Like, if he does indeed work for the NSA, what sort of work does he commonly do? Where's he come from? Where'd he train? Military service? Stuff like that. Can you do that?" Pause. "Great. Okay. Just fax back whatever you have, and I'd appreciate it." Pause. "Actually, they don't fish all that much up here. They milk cows, mostly." He smiled. "You get this for me and next time you come up, we'll milk some real swollen ones." Pause. "Great. Goodbye." Leland clicked off. He looked around his 'summer camp cabin'.

It was hard to believe the only free space in town was the motel room just vacated by their prime suspect, but there it was. Carmella offered it up as a sort of "Oops! Sorry." acknowledgement. And since it looked better than a swivel office chair would, out in the street on wheels, Leland took it.

Ralph Bunch had fashioned a nice handmade sign which read

"Sheriff's Office", and fastened it over the door. The place had a heavy iron bed, which they could handcuff someone to for a rudimentary jail.

Some lawmen drank to relax. Leland went home and laid down. Since summer had begun, it had been in the wicker sofa out on his screened-in porch. But not being home, he decided he'd try out the jail's bunk.

The first thing Leland considered, upon lying on his back to think, was that his killer, 'Stan', probably laid on this same bed and maybe in the same position doing the same thing. And they probably stared up at the same light fixture in the same ceiling. And neither one of them was going to clean that bug carcass fallen inside of the frosted glass light globe. It was too piquant.

Then he wondered how everyone was making out up there at Ramey's house. He had to catch a ride up there on the sly, somehow. Probably with Merlin. Then, he was fast asleep and having a lovely dream featuring Agent Hailey, which he clung to with all his might, despite, for some reason, being tossed back and forth roughly.

Leland woke to find Peter Barnett with his hands on him.

Sheriff Leland and Mayor Pete

"Sheriff."

"Mayor." Leland raised himself stiffly.

"What have you done with my town?" Peter asked, dropping the latest edition of the New York Times across his stomach.

There, in a quarter panel just below the fold, was printed:

"What the Hell is Happening to Kimmel County?" Asks Citizen

Recent events in sparsely populated Kimmel County currently have citizens scratching their heads. Two women are murdered and decapitated. On June 13th a local Kimmel couple from a well-known local dairy family died in a shoot out with the law. Above is the AP photo of a bewildered and obviously shell-shocked Officer Leland Kelly picking himself up off the main street of Kimmel, after his offices exploded Monday mid-morning, rolling a van load of Japanese tourists end over end and through the front window of a hardware store."

(Article continued with more photos on back page.)

Peter gestured Leland to stand up, which became an offered hand up.

Leland waved it off and stood. He offered the mayor his chair. The mayor politely refused.

Leland shook his head.

"What the hell happened?"

"You haven't heard a thing?"

"There's a blackened spot where your digs used to be. I'd guess they haven't come down yet?" Peter said.

Leland frowned.

"Just a joke. Probably not the time. But, really, what the hell has been going *on* around here?"

Leland opened his mouth to speak, but Mayor Pete continued.

"I just got in and Carmella was kind of mum - for once,

wouldn't you know it?" Mayor Pete's brows rose. "Which kind of got me worried, more so than even the vanished jail, I'd have to say."

Leland started to frame a response.

"Which, by the way, you needn't worry about." Mayor Pete turned to glance out the door towards where the jail would have been and began pacing. "I've got the funds arranged for a much newer and better jail anyway. And when we add that to the insurance monies, I'd go as far as to predict a bigger, newer, completely up to date facility with a couple new sheriffs' vehicles and possibly a deputy to boot." Peter strode back and forth, describing his vision. "So. Perhaps this will all be a good thing. So what do you think about that?

Leland thought that their mayor was definitely a manic/depressive who was currently climbing right out his regular hypomania in to a full blown episode.

"This place is on the brink of becoming the go to recreational area for busy business clientele, and other high rollers!" There was so much to be done. When Leland didn't answer, Peter halted. "There wasn't anyone hurt, by the way, was there? I mean, I'm just realizing now… I wasn't here, by the way. You'll have to forgive me, but I just got back bearing some really, good news."

Leland glared.

"So. It's hard, you know, to just sort of come down." Peter's face fell. "Okay. So maybe I'll sit down. What happened? I mean, *besides* our jail missing."

So Leland brought out two paper cups. Gave Mayor Pete his, to drop a couple of his lithium tablets into, and told him.

Mayor Pete thought about what Leland told him, after polishing off two Dixie cupfuls of water and several other pills. "Well. The Japanese tourists; they came here for the crime and violence, so I'd guess they got their money's worth. Lots to tell back home! I don't really see that hurting our tourist business. Your missing people are another problem, of course." Peter stuck his cup out asking for more.

"Of course." Leland frowned, pouring.

"I can't see that the city has any real exposure on this, but we can shove it past the lawyers. We'll see how that shakes out when we find them. We're on that, right?"

"Yes," Leland said.

"And as for Carmella. I suppose I'm gonna have to talk to her about it." Peter grimaced, as he thought about what Leland had said, and crushed his Dixie cup. "We have an 'open' marriage, as you may know Leland. But she really needs to screen some of these males she brings back to these cabins. If, for no other reason, than she could get hurt." Pete looked concerned. "She's never had real good taste in men. I mean, other than myself." He flushed. "Freedom to choose is not a *license* to grub around with every Tom, Dick and Harry who drifts through. I've tried to make this plain to her, Leland."

"I'm sure you have, Pete." Leland nodded.

Pete nodded in return. "Well, I've got to go. Keep me in the loop."

"It's more like a figure eight, lying on its side, and wriggling like a tapeworm. ...but you're involved." Leland smiled.

Mayor Pete shook his head and left.

Leland Calls on Merlin

"Hey! You made the Times again, you big celebrity you," Merlin said to Leland upon picking up the phone.

"Yeah." Leland grunted, folding the spread pages back.

"Hope you're saving the clippings. I usually toss the Times out with the fish in three days. But this will all be important months from now when you go before the council for a larger budget - and maybe years from now when the history of Kimmel is written and *your* name figures prominently," Merlin's voice rose.

"I can feel the heat of your jealousy from here Merlin," Leland said.

"Well, I have been ruminating over the fact that veterinarians risk their health and well-being every day in unsung ways tending to the lame and the ill."

"How would you like to maybe risk your health and well-being dealing with your government?"

"I feel that I do that already, every day, Leland."

"That's what I thought you'd say Merlin, which is why you're my boy."

"I'm your boy" for *what*, Leland?"

"For getting to the bottom of what amounts to some crazy shit happening around here of late."

"I was wondering when you'd ask. ...again."

"Can you pick me up? I've lost my ride," Leland said.

"Be right there," Merlin answered.

Merlin drove up a few minutes later in his old weathered Ford Explorer, which tended to fling shit from the tire sides when he reached speeds greater than 25 mph. Leland hopped in and they drove back to the veterinary clinic. Merlin's brows rose as he said, "You have some actual cow shit for me to look at this time?"

He parked where Leland asked him to in the back.

"No. I just want to visit a little inside, if that's okay," Leland said.

"It's fine, Leland. Love the human company," Merlin said, ushering him in after unlocking the back door.

They walked in and around and settled in Merlin's office. Merlin poured them a couple cups of coffee.

"Thanks." Leland nodded.

"So whatcha got?" Merlin settled himself.

"Well. For one, I believe we've caught our killer." Leland smiled.

"You're kidding me."

Leland shook his head. "Got a positive ID and our man. Though it's nothing I believe would stand up in court."

"Congratulations." Merlin leaned forward resting his elbows on his knees. "Why won't it stand up in court?"

"I'll show you why in a bit. But I've got another problem that needs working on now."

"Don't tell me." Merlin waved. "You're wondering why your Sheriff's office blew up?" Merlin smiled slightly. "You're figuring it was more than the fumes off a discarded bottle of Ruth's nail varnish."

Leland nodded. "You always had a good nose."

"That I have," Merlin agreed. "Comes from dealing with animals which can't talk to me, which I've always felt gave me a little edge in understanding people who won't." Merlin scrutinized Leland. "You got ...any suspects? I mean, you must have someone more in mind besides the person whom you've already arrested."

"Yeah," Leland admitted. "And that's why I'm concerned."

"You're ..."concerned". Merlin pondered. He settled back and the smile left his face.

They both took time to sip their coffee. Merlin was thinking that they were now sitting in another building - *his* - which conceivably could *also* blow up.

"Now you're making *me* 'concerned', Leland."

"Maybe *we* should be," Leland admitted.

"You want to fill me in a little further?" Merlin asked. He studied Leland as Leland appeared to hesitate. "Maybe issue me a gun?"

"Yeah, but I think now is a good time to go." Leland nodded and rose towards the door.

Merlin sighed. He set his coffee and rose.

"Let's leave our cell phones here," Leland said.

"Off the grid, huh." Merlin surrendered his cell. "Or you scared of sparks?"

"Not so much sparks," Leland said, stopping outside of the door to look up.

"The weather doesn't change much around here in twenty minutes, Leland," Merlin observed.

"Nope," Leland agreed, scanning the skies.

…"Drones?"

Merlin shook his head.

Leland couldn't say as he saw any. But that didn't necessarily mean anything.

Here We All Are

"Here we all are," Ruth said.

There were seven of them in all: Leland, Merlin, Ruth, Agent Hailey, Nancy Gillis, Stan and Ramey; eight, if you counted Ramey/Muffin Lady as two. And all crammed into Ramey's basement. A more paranoid bunch would have been hard to find in Kimmel County. They had all removed the batteries from their cell phones and locked them in Ramey's lead lined safe. The Sheriff's car had been hidden. The blinds of the basement windows had been drawn. They were in Ramey's basement, so as to hide heat signatures from overflying drones (Stan's idea), and clustered around Stan (not Stan's idea).

"Since when have we all joined the Tea Party?" Agent Hailey shook her head, gazing around the cinderblock basement walls.

"I think it happened just after our government tried to blow you all up," Merlin suggested.

"Says our Serial Killer," Agent Hailey pointed out.

Leland nodded.

"A makeshift bomb using a propane bottle and surgical tubing would seem to be just the sort of device you had been trained to use." Leland eyeballed Stan.

"True," Stan admitted.

"This Perez fellow, who came to see me, seems to know pretty much all about you and your training, and has the forensics to back it up," Leland continued.

"Oh, and I'm sure that if you put the battery cables to *him*, he could tell you *a lot more* about me and my training, than even *I* know." Stan grimaced sourly.

"I say we use the battery cables right now and see how much more *he* knows!" The Muffin Lady shrieked. Ramey was striding back and forth at the perimeter, breathing heavily, and looking for an opening in.

"Just to put you on notice, Merlin. Nancy - our dead 'Muffin

Lady' here - is currently inhabiting Ramey's body, which recently cold cocked our perp here with a shovel just before the jail blew up." Leland had already gotten Merlin up to speed on most of the matter on the drive up.

"Umm," said Merlin, as if diagnosing an animal who had been eating locoweed, and sized Ramey up.

"Merlin. This is Nancy Loomis." Leland introduced him. "Ms. Loomis. This is Merlin, our local veterinarian."

"Nice to meet you," Merlin said. He stuck out his hand. …"Sorry for your loss," he added, as if it might have been something for them both to regret.

Ramey's snort made Merlin wince.

Stan shook his head where he sat, back to the wall. "Women," he snorted. "You can't live with 'em, and you can't kill 'em." He nodded towards Ramey/Muffin Lady. "Frankly, I'm open to suggestions."

"I suggest we hang him by his balls!" The Muffin Lady raged.

"You know how I found you?" Stan spit. "I just turned my head like a radar dish, and it picksed out the biggest ball buster around. And you frankly, took the… muffin, I suppose. You were Code Red all in candles. You were knocking all of the other signals around here right off the band! I started picking you up as your Mercedes with the buttery calves' leather interior topped the knoll coming out of Seattle and up over the ridge in Eastgate. And by the time you reached Kimmel you were a full-fledged migraine."

"And I'm supposed to feel bad about that?"

Stan opened his mouth to reply. Then looked as if he had decided to say something else. "You know, this all wouldn't have happened if you were, *or just tried to be*, a nicer person," Stan suggested, "and investigated your feminine side."

Merlin about bust a gut laughing at that.

"Oh for God's sakes, Sheriff. How much more of this fellow do

I have to take?" Ramey gestured as if a line side coach leaning in across the line of scrimmage, aghast at an umpire's call. "Why am I having to repeat? I am the victim here!"

Things had a way of escalating within their small group, Leland could see.

"You know, I think if we all get some chairs and just sit," Leland said, "take a few breaths, and see if we can't get our minds around a few things. Things might go better." He smiled.

"I'm way ahead of you there, Sheriff." Stan observed.

"That you are," Leland said, stepping in and pivoting from his hips and walloping Stan with a hard right to the face. "But the idea here is that we are going to catch up!"

The group froze. Leland looked around while breathing hard. Stan spit out a tooth.

Leland slowly recovered. Then he seated himself. "So why don't you tell us what you know?"

"Don't you want to Mirandize me? Offer me a lawyer or something?"

Leland said nothing.

Do *before* and *after* photos of the beatings?..."

"No."

"I can't see how this is ever going to trial then," Stan offered.

"Me neither," agreed Leland.

Stan looked around. Agent Hailey was poker faced. Stan turned to her. "Don't you federal people take an oath, or something?"

"Yeah. And we sometimes go to church, too."

"I see," Stan said, after a while.

"The first thing you've got to understand," Stan began, "is that I'm just as much a pawn in this game as you are." He glanced around but found no sympathy. "This isn't checkers, though. You can't double jump and get king'ed. You start out a pawn and you don't move up."

Leland moved his chair closer.

"You have to understand that much of what I have to say is hearsay and supposition." He eyed Leland.

"He's afraid he might mislead us," Agent Hailey shook her head.

"No," Stan countered. "I *will* mislead you. It's the fog of war. No one knows what is going on. *Even the people we're hiding from.* The shit has hit the fan, man!"

"I don't follow."

"Look at him - or *her.*" Stan indicated Ramey. "Minds are moving around willy nilly now. They're not sticking with their bodies. Shit. That guy the other night in the bar? His head is infested with a chipmunk! You *noticed* that, right?"

Leland nodded slightly. "Ralph's always been a little squirrelly."

Stan laughed, shook his head. "The shit is outta the box now and hoppin' around in the woods! And as far as I can see there's no putting it back. Though they're still out there trying."

"You mean, the people who tried to blow us up."

"Yeah. Them and the people who tried to blow *me* up, also."

Agent Hailey moved in. "Could you mean there's more than one group of people trying to kill us?"

"Who knows?! …is what I'm saying." Stan shrugged his shoulders. "In an operation as big as this, there's usually lots of players." Stan nodded repeatedly. "There's invariably leaks, and then others join in, trying for the gold…"

"Oh fuck," Merlin swore.

"Merlin." Leland nodded towards Nancy Gillis.

Merlin glanced at Nancy, and then back at Leland. "You're kidding, right? This is going in the *Times*, Leland?"

Ruth shook her head.

Merlin's brows rose.

"Maybe we all ought to begin at the beginning," Leland said. "Ramey? Perhaps you and Nancy here and Ruth could run upstairs and hustle us up something to eat and drink. I think Stan is a little hungry and it is around mealtime and this might take us a while."

"He thinks he can torture me for the truth," Stan declared to them all. "But first off, I've got no reason not to tell you everything I know. And second, I've had an operation on my brain that makes torture entirely ineffective. In fact, it stimulates me. Just getting this tooth knocked out has made me feel more alive than I have in months for example." Stan grinned a gap toothed grin.

"He's lying," Ramey said.

Stan smiled at her. "Hit me. C'mon, hit me!"

"You f&cking piece of moisturized fecal matter! …"

"I'm not going anywhere," Nancy Gillis declared over her notepad. "And you've about as much chance of getting me out of this room… as you do of turning Carmella Burnett into a virgin!"

"Nancy Elizabeth Gillis!" Ruth declared.

"You know," Merlin interjected. "You have about the same chance of the Pope granting Carmella Burnett an *indulgence* as you would have of getting the New York Times to publish any of this we're hearing now."

"I've had two pieces run already, front page!" Nancy said adamantly.

"Yes, but *now* - even if it were true - it's too far-fetched. What we're hearing now would undermine their credibility, actually anyone's credibilty. They simply can't publish something as far out as this - true or not." Merlin regarded Nancy kindly. "Can you see that?"

Nancy said nothing.

Merlin flourished his hands as he walked circles staring at the ceiling and gathered his thoughts. "Okay. Okay, Nancy. Say everything you tell them is absolutely true! Maybe you even garnish it with a few of the beatings and add the torture. If they publish it, the story will not be the one you are sending them. The story will be about why the New York Times seems to have gone off the deep end all of a sudden in publishing this wild fiction from a formerly unknown, teenage reporter? Now *there's* a story with *legs*. And one which all of the Time's competitors would pick up and run with in a heartbeat."

Merlin circled.

"And that's all it would be about for weeks! And by the time the story *may* be proven to be true - and there's a good chance it won't and will go down buried in the annals of history right next Roswell and Area 51. By that time… the New York Times has lost *all* of its credibility *and* its audience."

Merlin addressed them all. "You see how the incentives are stacked here? *People think that they are reading all of the news of the day. But there is actually a very, narrow window of information that any media source can publish.* And *that* depends upon their readership. The New York Times is read by people who regard themselves as intelligent and important and most of all *see reality clearly.* And these sorts of people don't stick their necks out. They are not missionaries. They don't read shit like this. If they get it on them, it's social napalm. It burns! When these people see the National Enquirer they look the other way, as if they'd met the homeless or been caught shopping at Cost for Less. They don't talk shit like this. And they sure as hell don't read it or repeat it."

"Your language, Merlin."

"People *can not stand* too much reality," Merlin insisted. "Carl Jung, the pioneering psychologist said that. And by the way, animals can stand *much* more."

"That's *enough*, Merlin," Ruth said.

"No. No. If she's going to play in the big leagues, it's important she learn the game," Stan advised.

"Shut up, depraved killer," Ramey hissed.

All of the others agreed.

Nancy had stopped taking notes and was looking more and more depressed and angry as she considered Merlin's words.

"Merlin. I hope there's an upside to this little diatribe of yours, other than crushing the hopes of a small girl, while airing an old obsession." Leland frowned.

"There is." Merlin held up his arms as if revealing the git and smiled. "There *is* a ray of hope here."

"And in a basement, no less," Ruth observed.

"And it takes you out of the problem of undermining the Sheriff here, Nancy," Merlin said.

Nancy blushed, as if her traitorous thoughts had been bared to all.

"If you were to tell the Times that you were holding back further publication in lieu of publishing a book about the whole matter, and asked if they could suggest a publisher - chances are they would jump at the opportunity and ask for first serial rights to do so."

"So I withhold all of this to be put into a future book…" Nancy repeated.

Merlin nodded. "For which the publisher gives you a fat advance! You take time off from school to write it, while supporting your family with the advance. You put your dad in rehab. The Times publicizes it as an upcoming serialization. And you take upon your back the problems of credibility but get a lot more money, and a lot more editorial freedom."

"So I have to smother the story."

"No," Merlin said. "You just have to protect it until it has grown big enough to survive on its own and be told, before being killed. Because eventually - if you don't - that's what will happen."

A tear started down Nancy's cheek.

"I like it," Nancy decided finally, sniffing, but raising her head proudly.

"Well aren't we a happy bunch." Stan declared, air hissing through his missing tooth. "It's too bad we're all going to be dead soon."

The World According to Stan

"Okay. I give. Why are we all going to be dead pretty soon?" Leland asked Stan after Ruth and Ramey had left to prepare their dinner.

"Oh, let me think," Merlin broke in. "There's the seven… eight of us here holed up in a dentist's basement - on this side. And then on the *other* side - there's the entire resources of *our Federal Government?*"

Currently Merlin found himself clinging to his mortality. He was thinking how 'strange it was you never really considered whether or not you *really* wanted to be alive from day to day. You just woke up each morning and got on with your duties. But it wasn't like you had really 'taken the pledge.' Now Merlin was feeling the first inklings of being *really committed*. And he couldn't say he really liked it.

Stan nodded.

"Oh, but *also* on our side, I forgot to mention, the full resources of the Kimmel County Sheriff's Department. I'd forgotten that. Not to mention my quite costly - meaning, you will be billed if I ever survive this - veterinary advice," Merlin added glumly.

Stan smiled.

"Not to belittle the Kimmel County Shiriff," Stan insisted through his whistling tooth, "or this man's fine veterinary advice. But you also have *me*."

Leland's brows rose.

"I'm really the one chip you've got in this game Shirlock. And whether we all live - or we all die - will mostly depend upon how you decide to play me." Stan evaluated Leland's look. "You kill me now, and you lose this chip." Stan smiled, like a glint of gold.

"He's got a point Leland," Merlin said.

"So," Leland said, evaluating Stan. "According to you, that explosion in my offices was meant to kill *all* of us, not just you, and not just us."

Stan nodded. "It's the only time they would likely find us all together."

"Why would they want to kill you?" Leland leaned in to speak. "You work for them, right? That's why you carry this barcode on your forearm." Leland grabbed Stan's arm and turned it, revealing the underside and the bar code.

Merlin whistled.

"Isn't that so?"

"You ever hear of being fired? Or, of downsizing?" Stan waggled his head. "I'm a '*psycho*'. They aren't just going to let me walk free. I was useful to them as long as I was cleaning up their messes. But their messes are no longer 'cleanable'. Now it is time for them to distance themselves from what was a small problem to what has escalated for some reason to an *overwhelming* problem. So now there is nothing for me to do except to draw unwanted attention to them. Arrest me and scan my brain, and it opens a real can of worms. The sooner I'm six feet deep in the woods out there, somewhere, the happier someone I doubt I've ever met and probably never will, will be. And the better the school their kids will go to and the sharper the car they drive will be, probably, by the way."

"The happier 'who' will be?" Leland puzzled. "For all I'm sure of you set that blast, just as Agent Perez says. And you're some psychotic who has pasted a Wonder Bread barcode to his forearm and manufactured the delusion that all of your killing is in fulfilling a greater good in service to your government."

"You often notice in Law Enforcement," Agent Hailey who had been silent all of this time, broke in. "…that it often comes down to the fact that someone is *lying*."

"Wow." Merlin whistled. "There are so many sides to this."

Stan shook his head and stared at Leland.

"Yeah. I've noticed that also, Agent Hailey," Leland agreed.

Stan laughed. "I *like* her," he said, nodding. "You," he nodded at Leland, "not so much."

"And you," Stan noted Merlin, "are kind of a loose cannon."

Merlin didn't know how to take that.

"Fine. Let's do the good cop, bad cop, thing then," Agent Hailey said finally, drawing up a chair. Merlin found one for himself. And Nancy, who was transcribing all that she could, already had hers.

"Fine," Stan agreed.

Leland sat himself.

"I'm sure Stan has a very, good, and sensible reason for killing and decapitating the two women he did here in Kimmel County, and that given the opportunity to collect his thoughts and properly express himself will give us a cogent and sensible answer."

"You'd better believe it honey," Stan said, smiling.

"I can tell right off the bat that you two don't know shit about how the government works," Stan began, leaning towards Leland.

"No kidding." Merlin nodded.

Leland cast him a look.

"There is so much to tell, it's going to take me a few minutes just figuring out where to begin." Stan massaged his forearm bar code with his chin. "It tends to itch," he said.

"That means it's healing," Merlin noted. "And you've reason to worry, I've been trying to explain it to him for several years." Merlin indicated Leland.

Leland cast Merlin another look.

"You mean, to fabricate a plausible story?" Leland suggested.

Stan sighed, turning his attention to the stairs, down which Ramey was returning. "Oh, look. It's lunch."

The World According to Stan
(Part Two)

Leland spent his time frowning. Everyone ate their lunch quietly.

"It all didn't start out this way, huh?" Stan jerked on the handcuffs, after he'd had enough food. His wrists hurt. His head hurt. His jaw hurt. This was getting more real all the time.

"It all started out with me busting my ass to get into the Special Forces. Let me tell you, *that* ain't easy. You go through training harder than I imagine any of you would know about. They couple you with another jarhead. And between you there is this bellhop's chime which will make the training stop. Either one of you ring it - and you're both cut. I told the other guy that if he tried to go for that ringer I'd chop his hand off. He either was pretty tough, or he believed me, because we both made it. Then I shipped out for some sandy places I was told not to talk about. But I did find out a little bit about how modern guerrilla warfare is conducted, which might interest you."

They all looked at one another.

"And why is that?" Leland asked.

"Because that is what we are involved in right now," Stan answered. "The hallmark of guerrilla warfare is that the enemy is hiding in plain sight. At night the enemy attacks. Then the next day, the local chief motors in to discuss with you what went wrong. You tell them that you believe some of their troops allowed the rebels inside of the perimeters, and that you're not feeling too good about it! The local chief says he'll look into it. He does, and drags a couple grunts away. Maybe he shoots one or two, who of course are shouting that they are innocent - and very believably, you'd say. Weeks pass and the whole thing happens again. Finally, it happens that you see that one of the rebels you just killed was removed the month before. This is when you realize how guerrilla warfare works.

In the nighttime this chief is orchestrating the attack. The next day, he drops by to help 'clean up the mess'," Stan looked to Leland. "That is, to help 'get to the bottom of things'".

"So you're saying Agent Perez is actually in charge of suppressing this thing," Leland said.

"I think he wants to find out just who and what any of us knows, so that he can mop this whole operation up as aseptically as possible and to remove the taint of any government involvement before it all blows sky-high - which it's well on its way to doing. And he could really use your help in doing so."

"And we shouldn't help him because…?" Agent Hailey interposed herself.

"Because he doesn't represent *our* government. *You* represent our government. Just as I *used* to. But now I'm out here in no man's land," Stan declared. "I could say I was lured away through misrepresentation, but that really wasn't it."

"So you're saying there are these cells of individuals, having it both ways, within our government, who are working to overthrow our government?" Ruth asked.

"Hell no," Stan cried. "They don't want to overthrow *anything*. They *like* it just the way it is. All they are trying to do is to keep it *just the way it is*. That's what 'cleaning up this mess,' means."

Stan could tell he was losing people with his cross-purposes narrative. So he concentrated on 'saving his breath' for a while.

"Okay. And how is that? What is the way it is?" Leland asked.

"I think I can answer that one Leland, if you don't mind," Merlin spoke up.

Leland liked Merlin and Merlin was probably Leland's best friend, but Leland also knew that Merlin was often apt to let his thoughts run away with themselves. He had a tendency to let the string on his kite pretty far out. Leland sighed. "I suppose that as long as we're discussing the government, I expect that you're going to have to have your say Merlin.".

"As is my right as a citizen and taxpayer." Merlin nodded.

"We all pay taxes Merlin." Ruth yawned.

"You know, I pay *your* salary *plus* your taxes, so you might just want to listen to me also, if you want to stay in hairspray and nail remover," Merlin retorted. It wasn't good to get in bad with Ruth, but this was life and death, he reasoned.

"We *all* pay our taxes here, Merlin," Leland noted. "So get to your point."

"Certainly," Merlin pursed his lips. "What you all need to realize is that there are currently something like 20 million government employees and a total annual national operating budget of around 4 trillion dollars. And out of all this there probably no more than 50 or so government candidates and issues which you cast your one little vote on annually. In other words, *as a democratic nation we are a vast bureaucratic region just awash in money with virtually no oversight.* Just like all those warrens of terrorist activity in the Middle East where the enemy combatants blend in with their compatriots."

Leland shook his head like a dog as if to somehow shake off Merlin's misgivings, while the others worked hard at processing it.

"What do you do?" Stan asked him.

"I'm a veterinarian," Merlin answered.

"Huh."

" Huh?" Merlin's annoyance was visible.

"Let's move on," Leland suggested.

Stan nodded. "How about you, honey? " Stan asked Agent Hailey.

"I'm a Federal Officer," Agent Hailey said. "Which means - despite what Merlin, our veterinarian has said - I can't and *don't* do just whatever I want."

"That sounds good, like maybe you're waffling about killing me?" Stan replied.

Agent Hailey didn't reply.

"How about you? And you?" Stan turned to Ruth and Ramey.

Both gave him the thumbs down.

"Which leaves me with you, little girl. You ever seen a 'serial killer' before?"

"Not knowingly," Nancy Gillis replied. "Or you would've read about it."

Stan nodded.

"Well, look." Stan turned to them all. "You're all guilty of aiding and abetting a fugitive."

"Unless you disappeared," Merlin noted.

"You've been in my custody all the time," Leland said.

"You shared this with the Feds, did you?" Stan responded.

Then Muffin Lady then put in her two cents.

"What did I say?" Ramey asked, looking around. "What did I do?"

Nobody responded.

"Jesus! As the sole dentist around here I never got my due respect taking care of you all," Ramey swore. "And now, it's even worse!"

"It wasn't you, Doctor Ramey," Nancy Gillis said. "It was the Muffin Lady. She just recommended making shoes out of our prisoner's genitalia, and gloves of his facial skin. She also suggested that whatever further information we do get out of him should be done through the most heinously described torture. And I can see right now, that I'm going to have a harder and harder time painting her as a sympathetic character. So that I'm having to re-calibrate the narrative… as I've envisioned it, up until now, and probably the arc of my book."

"Yes. Well we all have our problems honey," Ruth advised. "What troubles me is that our serial killer here says we ALL are not going to be around much longer. I think we should ask him how he sees it that way? What do we know, other that we just caught the serial killer - who has tried to blow us up, besides? What's the point of getting rid of us? It seems to me, that would just be more bodies to explain away."

"You might be right," Stan said. "There is more you need to know."

"So they'll be sure to want to kill us," Ruth noted.

Stan smiled.

The World According to Stan
(Part III)

"You need to know how 'black ops' are run," Stan continued.

"Yes, I do," Nancy Gillis said.

"Yes. We certainly need to know about *that*," Agent Hailey said sarcastically.

"You are so sexy when you're pissed." Stan winked, or tried through a bruised face.

Leland gave him another roundhouse.

"Jesus. That felt good." Stan laughed, spitting out another tooth. "You keep this up Sheriff and you're gonna having to cut up my food."

"Maybe we'll puree *you*? Perhaps by running him through a hog?" Merlin suggested to Leland.

Leland was getting the feeling that this guy really genuinely *liked* pain. He smiled each time Leland punched him, which was an experience that aggravated Leland even more.

"You were lisping…" Agent Hailey nodded and smiled.

"Yeth. I wath." Stan nodded. "So ath I wath thaying…" He joked.

"Black ops aren't anything real mysterious. They are just government operations which we don't know anything about. Hell, the garbage collection around here is something I know nothing about." He indicated the need for a cigarette to Leland, and Ruth gave him a smoke. Merlin lit it. Stan nodded his thanks, and continued. "So, to me, your Sanitation Department hosts black ops operations. But, if I wanted to I could find out, just by going on the internet. So to me they are really grey ops; a very light grey ops."

"Now the sorts of 'black ops' you read of in the news are the darkest grey of the grey ops. The identities of the people involved in these operations are kept secret from most of our citizens, as is the financing, which is recorded under some very creative accounting schemes deep within the corridors of the CIA, or the NSA, or any of the other acronyms the public is vaguely aware of like EDGAR, and SAM, etc. But they are all responsible and accessible to known Senate committees and known public officials, like the CIA Director, etc. And, with the proper clearance, their budgets and operations can be known, by their legal overseers."

"A *true* black ops is *all* black, because it doesn't exist. And therefore it can't be 'found out'. It is a true guerrilla organization excepting that the ones which concern us don't want to take over power. They are something like dark matter. They are just *there*. All they want is to remain invisible and to keep on doing what they are doing."

"Which is *what?*" Leland asked.

"Which is *whatever they want to do.*" Stan smiled. "I mean, that's the point, isn't it?"

This had the group flummoxed.

Stan continued patiently. "We are talking about little domains which various parties have carved out within the bureaucratic infrastructure which suck their financing and operational needs and utilities and clearance from the government - but which the government as we know it, knows nothing of. There may be a lot of them. There may be a few of them. They may be doing good things. Or they could be doing bad. We don't know. They are totally black. Like a parasite which takes a little food from the host, without harming it in any measurable way is never detected - so these black operations go undetected. Actually, we might even call it commensalism, because it's in the best interests of all of these black ops to stabilize and grow the bureaucracy. Which by virtue of their very proliferation, they do. So they really stimulate the growth of our animal, the government. They are very pro-government."

"So running around the country murdering women and cutting off their heads isn't a problem for our government?" Agent Hailey asked sarcastically.

"When they are isolated events like this? Not at the Federal level." Stan nodded.

"I don't know why you are so shocked by all of this, Leland," Merlin spoke up. "Because what our serial killer here is detailing is just the logical extension of what I have been trying to tell you for years! You've got this huge, well-fed bureaucracy. It's just a petri dish for every sort of chicanery."

Leland sighed. He waved his hand at Stan. "You know what, just keep going."

So Stan did.

"It all starts, like anything, with someone who thinks outside of the box." Stan took a deep drag of the cigarette. "And it isn't very long before *thinking* something outside of the box leads to wanting to *do* something outside of the box. And this person is either already *within* the government and wanting to do something a little irregular. Or this person is *outside* the government and wants to do something a little irregular. But, whichever way it is, this person often has difficulty generating support."

"So, to illustrate how this support is arranged, let me begin with the simplest, warmest example I can bring to mind. There is this older matronly woman named Sylvia Phillips who loves to paint kittens. But she can't afford to. She has no time. She has lost her life savings due to a bad divorce and then medical bills, so she has to work a ten hour day behind the deli of a small grocery just in order to make ends meet. But she has a friend who thinks she is a genius, loves her paintings and who works for the government. So this friend gets her a job to serve as an outreach worker for a transient population in the area. She gets a car, a salary, medical care, and the chance to paint kitten portraits all day long. The friend gets bumped a salary upgrade since she is now supervising 20 people rather than 19. It's a win win."

"That's simple corruption," Agent Hailey countered, "and misdirection of federal monies. All of which are prosecutable felonies."

"Yup," Stan admitted. "*if* you ever get caught. But then lots of things are prosecutable. Did you know that the average citizen commits *three* felonies a day? And then there are things which the prosecutor won't prosecute, for any number of reasons, including that his bosses want it so."

"Or there are things done which the people elected like, and so eventually, instead of being prosecuted for an offence, you end up with a pension and a position or are given a medal, or end up a professor with tenure. I mean, there is no end to the good things which can come from subverting the law." Stan laughed.

"See!" Merlin nudged Leland. "What did I tell you?"

"You're a damned murderer," Agent Hailey said.

"The law is only the law for the people who have to pay attention to it. You trespass on the freeway, and you're going to get either chased off or hauled away. You trespass on the freeway because you're against **racism** with 10,000 other people who say they feel likewise - and the mayor of the city will come out and shake your hand!"

"This sort of thinking is so *corrosive*," Ruth festered.

"People can only stand so much reality," Merlin clucked.

"Ruth, he's a *serial killer*," Nancy Gillis reminded her.

"Well, yeah!" Ruth snorted.

Ramey hadn't anything to say. So Leland figured he was probably kept busy keeping the Muffin Lady's front door shut.

Stan smiled. "So you've got some interesting research you'd like to do, but the University committee has put the kibosh on it? Sell it to the Department of Defense, or the NSA, or the CIA - or even the Chinese. Whoever will help you to do what you want to do!" Stan smiled. "If it all works out, they can create some sort of serendipitous research back story in order to bring it out legally. And if it doesn't work out… well, it never happened."

"Because, in the end, this is what we all want. We all want to get to where mankind is eventually going to get to like it or not - except sooner! And this is why all of this can go on. *Because secretly all of us want this to happen."*

Stan glanced around the room. "We all want to be safe and secure. We all love our conveniences. And we all want our little Herby to be able to walk again, or to breathe again, or to live again - and if ten thousand people have to die or several have to be murdered to make these happen, we can live with it, if it's conducted in the proper manner and out of sight. Kind of like butchering cattle or killing chickens."

"I am actually, I would suppose, a free-lancer, tacitly employed by other institutions altogether... but whose activities are all coordinated on a server. So that if the shit ever hits the fan, I never existed. And you?" Stan regarded Leland. "Depends I would suppose on how much you know, and how good you can make the man *who runs me* feel about that."

It took a while for people to chew this over.

"So..." Leland was the first to speak. "Whose bright idea were *you?"*

Stan finished the cigarette and ground it out.

"In my case it was somebody over in the sandy climes of Pakistan working on 'synesthesia'."

Leland shook his head, as if the shit just wouldn't stop. And Stan didn't stop.

"There is no *there, there.* All of these black ops entities are only hierarchies in a server somewhere. All of their employees are hired elsewhere, though other government services, where they are purportedly doing something else. So there is no budget. There is no payroll. And there is no *there,* there or here!" Stan laughed. "Who am I? Why, I'm *nobody.* Or perhaps I'm somebody, supposedly up a river in Africa taking water samples."

"The government is just honeycombed with shit like this," Merlin agreed.

"It's a fine story," Leland said. "How many people here think it's time to shoot him?"

Most everybody raised their hand including Ramey.

But Merlin objected.

"Just wait a minute Leland," Merlin demurred. "He mentioned synesthesia."

"Yeah?" Leland removed the big Anaconda from its holster on his hip. He placed the big gun on his knee and began loading it with bullets. "That's a real thing? Like a real word?" He laughed.

"Yes it is." Merlin scrutinized Stan, moving closer, examining Stan's cranium. "And I'd be interested in whatever our serial killer here has to say about it. It *looks* as though he might have been experimented on himself."

"Which would give him grounds for an insanity plea." Agent Hailey nodded.

"This weapon will blow holes in any insanity plea," Leland said.

"Now just hold on a minute, Leland," Merlin said, looking up from the scar he was tracing through the back of Stan's scalp.

"Leland, you know that I can't let you just execute a wanted fugitive," Agent Hailey replied.

"We'll just see how the thing plays out. How's that?" Leland said, gripping his loaded Anaconda.

"You need to think this through," Stan said. "If you shoot me, how does this affect the chances of the other people in this room?"

"Were you experimented on?" Merlin asked.

Stan gazed around at the room of them, most of whom wanted him dead.

"Yes," Stan replied.

"Well?" Leland raised the tip of the gun.

"As it happened," Stan said. "We ran over a mortar in Afghanistan, and I took some shrapnel in the old rock. They airlifted beyond our base hospital to a facility which was a lot newer, and cleaner and technologically quite superior - from what I could make of it - from any of the outpost facilities I was used to. Bunkered inside of a hill I discovered later. Lots of money put into this, and a low profile."

"I wasn't thinking at my best and worried about the possible outcome of my injury. It was hard to do certain things. And they weren't very optimistic about my outcome either. Until one day this new doctor walks in and says he thinks he can fix it so that I'll be an even better soldier than before. I said that was kind of hard to believe. But what kind of soldier doesn't want to hear this?" Stan glanced around. "So I say, 'Sounds like just the thing.'"

"He says it will involve a bit of an operation. But hell, they're going to be digging around in my head anyway for that shrapnel, so I couldn't see as how a little more could be that bad. He explains a little bit about it, and the word 'synesthesia' plays a large part. As he told it, in 'synesthesia' parts of the brain can either increase in abilities when other parts are eliminated, or they can take over the jobs of those other portions… which can lead to many unforeseen conditions - or *unleash unknown abilities*, as he explained it to me. And he told me about autistics and idiot savants, and a lot more than I could grasp. But what I did grasp was that if I signed all these papers, that at the end of it all I'd have a shot, which was all I wanted. So I signed. And in I went."

"And what happened?" Merlin needed to know.

"Well. Here. Let me show you," Stan said, putting his hands out. "You got a toothpick?"

As Stan began flexing his hands, pumping his fists actually, Merlin looked to Leland. Leland considered the gun in his hand and nodded Merlin his assent. Merlin gave Stan a toothpick.

Stan took the toothpick between his thumb and forefinger and spoke, as he poked one end of the toothpick into the handcuff keyhole. "There's something very interesting about having an ability that far exceeds whatever the current reach of that ability is." Stan's fingers began to move very quickly and then to vibrate. "Most of our defenses are unknowingly crafted from within our own existing parameters. So for example, you want to keep deer out of your garden? You erect an 8' hogwire fence. But what if a deer comes along who can leap 20'?" The toothpick vibrated almost imperceptibly with a high pitched faint hum like a dentist's drill, until, suddenly the handcuffs sprung apart. "See?"

Everyone shrunk back as Stan thrust his freed hands forward.

Except for Leland who held the 44 in a very steady gun hand with it trained on Stan.

"You think it would be a good idea for me to shoot him now?" Leland asked Agent Hailey.

"These handcuffs cannot be 'picked' - but they can be 'vibrated'." Stan tossed them off to the side. "Just a bar trick." Stan rested his hands on his knees. "But you get my point?"

Merlin nodded.

"This seems to be solving my moral problem Leland," said Agent Hailey, who had her gun drawn also.

"Yeah." Nodded Leland who slowly increased the pressure on the trigger as he backed and encouraged the others to back away also.

"So whatever they did caused you to be able to move very fast?" Merlin ventured.

And in that moment, Stan leapt. He was already clear of that spot on the wall where Agent Hailey's bullet embedded itself. And before Leland could squeeze off a shot, Stan had knocked the gun barrel upwards. The massive bullet plowed through the floor/ceiling. Then by twisting the barrel, Stan tossed Leland as he stepped in and wrenched the gun free at the same time. Leland somersaulting onto his butt with his back to the wall. Stan had the big gun trained on Agent Hailey before she could complete her turn.

"No!" Leland screamed.

Agent Hailey froze in mid-thought expecting death. She let her hand on the gun relax. It fell to the floor.

Stan smiled.

"Yes." Stan nodded to Merlin, as he sat back down after collecting Agent Hailey's gun. "The operation was a great success! I got amazing speed. I just love pain. It's almost a sexual thing, though it's a little creepy when put like that. And I don't mind killing people, at all. It's strange. It's like I have this bookish description of how the remorse should feel. But it's just not there. If anything, it's like a phantom limb which almost begs you to scratch it." He spoke thoughtfully as he swept the gun sight over them all and little beads of sweat broke out on his forehead. "Perhaps you can sense now, how hard of a time I'm having not pulling this trigger," Stan added.

We Do Things Stan's Way

"What are we doing now?" Nancy Gillis asked, after an hour had passed, and she'd finished catching up her notes.

"He's thinking. We're watching him think." Leland smirked. "He moves fast as anything. But then, sooner or later, it comes time to think."

Actually, they were watching him sweat. As Stan held the gun, at first it was if he were weighing it, imagining its action, eyeballing them and waving it from one of them to the other - looking ever more serious as he did so. It reminded Merlin of following the black ball on a roulette wheel. It was nerve-wracking as hell. Especially after Stan had begun to murmur and then mumble to himself, almost in argument, as he passed the gun from one hand to the other.

"You'd better handle this, for a moment," he said, slipping the grip of the gun from his right hand into his left palm.

Leland raised his brow at Agent Hailey.

"We should kill them all now."

Agent Hailey and Leland looked at each other, questioningly.

"You do that, and what have we got then?"

"Less variables."

"Dead people have less variables."

Ramey's Muffin Lady spoke out. "You can go ahead and kill *me*! I'm sick and tired of being a dentist."

Ramey placed both hands hard over his mouth as if he were about to upchuck and sped upstairs.

But it was as if Stan's hands hadn't even noticed, deadlocked as they were in an earnest conversation.

"You got a better idea?" Stan's right hand took the gun back.

"Not yet. And I'm feeling the need to kill something pretty soon."

"Well, let's just think about something else."

Time passed. You could hear the faint tick of the mantle clock.

"Like what? They're all sitting there, silent, looking at us. It's really getting to me. We could end that."

"Our days of cutting off heads are over. It just doesn't do any good no more."

Leland felt he heard a bit of a whine bleeding into Stan's voice, at least when he was in the 'character of his right hand'.

The gun began to slip from Stan's right hand into his left, as a new wave of sweat beaded his forehead. "No." His right hand suddenly swept the gun away. "I think we need to think some more about this! The Sheriff here is in communications with whoever it is runs us. Perhaps if we find some way of working together, we can negotiate some kind of palatable end for all parties."

"I can give us a 'palatable end' right now. Give it to me."

"No. We need to think. this. through. Here. Why don't we just put in on the coffee table right here in front of us while we consider the situation?"

"No. Give it to me!"

"No-ooo," Stan whined, but weaker this time. He shook his head like a dog, flinging the sweat off, as he moved to set the gun onto the coffee table.

"I said! GIVE ME THE GUN!"

His left was clearly the alpha hand.

They all sat transfixed as the disagreement between Stan's hands rose to a fevered pitch, as the right gun hand extended out of reach of the left.

"I'll take it!" Merlin suggested suddenly, as Stan's left hand made a grab for it..

Stan's right hand flicked the gun - as if he were tossing a hot coal - to Merlin, just as the left missed it.

"Well… That was easy!" Merlin noted to Leland, juggling the gun gingerly and backing far away with the business end pointed towards Stan.

The others took a deep breath and exhaled.

Stan looked completely deflated. His shirt and hair were soaked in sweat. His hands hung limp. He appeared groggy. Nancy Gillis took notes rapidly. Ruth conferred with Ramey and then returned with some duct tape, while Sheriff Leland and Agent Hailey visually consulted.

Merlin handed Leland back his gun.

Leland nudged the safety and slid the big Anaconda back into its holster. It had a fairly long barrel and he had to lift his arm a pretty good ways to do so. And while he did so, he considered what their next move might be,

Agent Hailey inspected her underarms, where her uniform shirt was sopped. She wrinkled her nose.

"We'll see how you are at vibrating your way out of this!" Ruth grinned deliciously, as she wrapped both Stan's wrists and ankles heavily with the duct tape. However, it was as if she were talking to the dead. Stan had either drifted into a coma or was dead asleep.

Maybe it was a coma. Because when Leland peeled back an eyelid, all that were revealed were the whites. His breathes still came out ragged though, and his pulse was strong.

Evan Cobb - Pinch, West Virginia

Colin Mayfield had Skype-interviewed several high school journalism students in the proximity of Pinch, West Virginia. But three were only interested in interviewing celebrities. Another was too tied up following the race for City Council, claimed he was already a press 'intern' and sounded as though he would want money. So that left Colin with the only other possibility, Evan Cobb, a whisp of a freshman with food in his teeth, a half full glass of milk setting by his computer, big thick glasses and a bowl cut, who claimed he did 'investigative journalism' and was "quite thorough". He also lived nearby the scene of where the incident had purportedly taken place and had a bike. He also claimed to have a "photographic memory".

Colin settled upon him and gave him all of the particulars along with the appropriate cautionary advice. Evan barely listened and said that he probably new West Virginia a lot better than Colin "ever would" and hung up.

Colin didn't quite know where that left him with Evan.

Evan knew right where he stood, however - or rather sat. He was in the back room of the Pinch, West Virginia Marshall's office looking for filed reports dating from the time around when the disappearing school bus incident had taken place. It had taken some persistence and quite some persuasion, but finally Ms. Sally Anne, the records clerk, had allowed him back room access on the premise of looking for his absent father. Evan had told the woman that his mother had been having trouble making ends meet. And that she had confessed while drinking alone one evening, in front of a particularly wrenching version of "Justified" on television, that Evan was the son "of a Federal Agent. Or, at least, that's what he said he was." Who had been in and around Pinch at the time of the school bus disappearance, "around the fall of 1986", Evan added. It sounded as if he were someone with a good job, Evan told Ms. Sally Anne. And he figured perhaps he could make things a little easier for his mom if he could find his father - and perhaps squeeze a little money out of him, by the way.

Ms. Sally Anne's brows bunched. "You're a little young to have been hatched then, aren't you?" She asked.

"Yes, I am. Actually, the affair continued on and off for many years," he admitted, reluctantly.

"There's no need to hang your head now. It was none of your doing," Ms. Sally Anne counseled.

"He was married."

Ms. Sally Anne shook her head.

"He finally left when my mom was pregnant with me."

Ms. Sally Anne's face hardened. "We'll just see what we can do about that," she nodded.

Evan didn't mention the school bus incident. He merely gave Ms. Sally Anne the month and year of the period through which he wanted to comb the files. He had figured any Federal Agent would come by and introduce himself to the local authorities as a matter of courtesy, and that a note should have been made of this meeting in the Sheriff's log.

Ms. Sally Anne was only too happy to oblige by then. Chasing down a philandering, deadbeat federal official seemed as good a use of city records as any to her!

Evan arrived after school that day and worked until closing hours. Then he returned, having taped the bolt of the self locking rear door open, and worked through the night powered by a quart of milk, two peanut butter sandwiches and an apple. By morning, he had his man: Special Agent Robert Purvis of the FBI, who could be reached at: area code 202 224 5987. Evan snuck out the back door. He heard it lock. Then he returned through the front entrance an hour later, after having coffee and a nut crusted cake donut across the street and thirty minutes before the start of school. He handed Ms. Sally Anne the I.D. information neatly printed out and asked if she would mind using the Sheriff's computer network to check it out. Ms. Sally Anne said that she would certainly try.

Evan was too keyed up and tired to pay much attention in school that day. When he finally returned to the Marshall's offices Ms. Sally Anne met him with a mixed look.

"I checked and re-checked all of the names in the FBI database as far back as 1980 and there are actually *three* Robert Purvis' shown as licensed FBI agents. The oldest, I'm afraid, is shown as having died in 1996. The other two it seems are still alive, although only one is still in the employ of the FBI. I've made copies of all three with their pertinent information. Here you go," she said quietly, and handed Evan the information. "I doubt that what I've done is proper, and I probably could be disciplined, so I'd appreciate you keeping this between us two."

Evan assured her that he would.

"But I don't care!" She added, wishing him the best as she closed the door.

Evan Cobb was elated. His impulse was to get this information off as quickly as possible and to see his byline in the Times! On further reflection however, he realized his job was as yet only half done. He looked over the FBI I.D. with photos of the three men. All three looked serious, effective and, actually, *honest*. But then the shadowy figure he was hunting would *appear* so. He had to figure out which one of these men was actually the agent who had investigated the school bus incident. He thought about how to do this on his bike ride home. He hoped that the agent was one of those two who were still living. He wondered how to find out which one. To trace them back by their worked assignments through the archived FBI files would require an access he couldn't imagine he'd ever acquire. But after he'd mulled the problem a while another way occurred to him.

When he got home he called the Charleston Gazette.

"Hello," he said. "I'm trying to locate a photographer who worked for the Gazette during the fall of 1986. I wonder if you could help me locate who that was?"

"Hold on, I'll send you back to the Art department."

Evan held.

"Hello!"

Evan repeated his request.

"Well, you certainly hit the big money with that request," the voice of an older man barked.

Evan asked him why.

"That would be me!" The voice replied. "Yes. I'm still alive."

Bonaparte P. Trenton

Bonaparte P. Trenton was the photographer's name. And Evan had to meet with him on a Sunday, as visiting required going all the way into Charleston for which Evan had to take the Greyhound. Evan woke at 5:30am that Sunday morning, packed a large sack of food, and bought a round trip ticket, at the coffee shop, for Charleston leaving at 8:00am sharp from in front of the Miner's Mercantile on Troy Street.

Evan arrived at Bonaparte's small cottage-sized home in Charleston by 12:30. He pressed the buzzer. For a long time he heard nothing and was very afraid that all of his trouble had been for naught. He was about to ring again, when the door cracked open. "Yeah?" The voice Evan remembered from his phone conversation replied.

"Mr. Bonaparte?"

"That's TRENTON! Bonaparte is my first name."

"Oh. Sorry. Mr. Trenton?"

"Yeah?"

"It's Evan Cobb. We spoke over the phone Wednesday."

"I can't begin to tell you how many people I have spoken with over the phone between now and this past Wednesday! Could you be more specific?"

"Yes I can."

"Well do so," the man replied before Evan could speak further. "Can't you see how busy I am?"

'Well, no, I can't,' Evan thought. "And for a number of reasons," he mumbled, talking into the crack.

"What was that?"

"I'm the boy who wanted to talk to you about some photographs you took back in October of 1986."

There was a long pause.

"Oh, *that* boy." The door widened further. "The one with the deadbeat dad?"

Evan nodded.

The first thing Evan noticed was that Bonaparte P. Trenton was in dirty striped pajama bottoms. The second thing Evan noticed was that a cigarette hung from his lower lip as if it were taped there. Its ash was at least an inch long.

"Well, come on in," he ordered. The ash fell off his cigarette.

Evan entered.

The front room was remarkably neat and tidy. Around the room were numbers of large framed glossies of news photos. "I took all those," Bonaparte remarked as he strode through the room and Evan followed.

"I always felt there was something just a little off about that fella," Mr. Trenton said, as they reached a back bedroom which apparently was an archival area. A pasteboard box labeled 1986 set on a card table. Mr. Trenton threaded a roll of negatives through an illuminator. "You were right to think I'd have a lot of extra shots of the school bus investigation. Less than one percent of what a photographer will shoot ever sees the light of day… anywhere. Nevertheless, I usually keep them all. You never know the questions which will arise, like right now. I remember that guy clearly, because he obviously didn't want his picture taken. Later, he came up to me and asked if I could refrain from taking any shots of him and destroy any shots I already had? Said it was on account of his working undercover at times and a federal matter."

"Not all that unusual a request, you might say, for a law enforcement official?" Mr. Trenton continued parsing the negatives. "Here we go."

Evan followed the images on the wall. It was as if Mr. Trenton, the photographer, were chasing a shadow. First he disappeared behind another's face. Then he was a dark silhouette in a crowd. Then, he was too far away and blurry to be recognizable. "I think that it was the way he said it that got my back up. Decided I had to get a good shot of him, whether he liked it or not. Didn't see what harm it could do, if it were only for my own use."

"Finally got a good one, close up, in good light by using my wide angle lens. He figured I was shooting what was out in front of me, which I was. But the wide angle gave me almost a 180 degree perspective. And here he is…"

Mr. Trenton brought the face up and enlarged it. It was very clear, in good light with fair shadowing. Evan studied the photo. It wasn't anyone he had seen at all.

"You don't look happy," Mr. Trenton observed.

Evan took the FBI photo copies from his back pocket and showed them to Mr. Trenton. "Does he look anything like these guys to you?"

Mr. Trenton wiped his glasses carefully, then held the photos up into the light and beside the image on the wall. He shuffled through all three. "No, he don't."

Evan nodded.

Evan thought about the ramifications of this for a while, while Mr. Trenton kept his silence.

"Could you make me a print of that negative?" Evan asked.

"I sure could," Mr. Trenton said. "How big you want it?"

"Letter sized?"

"Shouldn't be a problem."

"How much would that cost?" Evan asked.

"Well, I usually give out the first one for nothing," Mr. Bonaparte Trenton lied.

"I would like one then. And thank you."

Mr. Trenton nodded.

After the photographer had made the print, dried, and slid it carefully into a manila envelope for transport, he handed it to Evan as he stood in the doorway.

"Hope this hasn't been too big of a disappointment," Mr. Trenton said, as he nodded his goodbye to Evan.

"No. No, you know. It is what it is." He gave Mr. Trenton what his best guess at what a brave smile would be.

"It makes sense you know, that if he was the sort to lie about the rest of it, he'd lie about being a Federal Agent too."

Evan nodded.

"The real question - at least about the Federal Agent part - is why?"

Evan agreed.

"And to that, I have no answer." Bonaparte Trenton, the photographer, shook his head and closed the door.

Evan nodded.

All the way home on the bus Evan considered this.

Benny Visits Kimmel

It wasn't more than one minute past when the sign announced "Entering Kimmel", than Bennie Green and his nephew, Duane, had driven right smack dab through the heart of it. Bennie slowed and took the air. It was pretty much as he had expected, here and there the scent of hay and cow manure, the heaviness of air and soil with moisture in it and lots of forest. And once inside the city limits, he smelled the Café blowing off its essence of weak coffee, bacon, and the breakfast special with a couple trucks parked outside. He had heard that rural people tended to do things earlier in the day, so he had made it a point to arrive here by breakfast time. His plan was to meet with the mayor, Peter Barnett, of this little burg and to get their project off of the ground. One reason Bennie had brought Duane along was that there was also a lot of money in the trunk.

Before he pulled into a slot before the Campaign Café though, Benny thought he'd take a moment or two to survey the town. He motioned for Duane to keep driving and to do a two block circle of the Café before parking. In passing, he noticed the blackened area with a few collapsed walls where the Sheriff's offices had been. He'd read about that. Curious business. Maybe he and the Sheriff ought to have a talk also, Bennie considered. Size the fellow up.

Duane tooled around. There wasn't much to make of it, just the normal stuff. Bennie wondered where the Sheriff was keeping himself now. In a few minutes Duane had made a complete circuit and Benny was back in front of the Café. So he directed Duane to pick a slot and park, and then they walked in. Their waitress wasn't a hooker, but Bennie guessed she could be a talented amateur. The name embroidered on her well-filled blouse said "Carmella". Benny asked Carmella if the owner, Pete, were around. She looked a little shaken by his words. But she motioned them to a booth and assured Bennie she'd "find him!"

They got a few looks. Bennie was plainly 'city'. But it was really Duane they were all gazing at. Duane was 6'9" and weighed about

380. Plus, with huge features and an unshaven mug, he was about the ugliest thing you'd seen on feet. Duane glanced around, and they all dipped their heads and returned to their meals. Bennie smiled slightly.

Peter Barnett appeared.

"What's good here?" Bennie looked up to ask.

Peter Barnett was wearing a half apron and walked up to Bennie with all of the confidence his quaking legs could muster and said, "Here. Let me walk you through the menu."

"That's nice of you." Bennie nodded.

"It's my pleasure. Are you looking for a light brunch, or a more filling, farmer's meal? We offer quite a selection of both."

"Well, I think we'd like both," Bennie replied. "Something a little French, with meat and a croissant for myself. But my nephew here, Duane, would probably like a larger portion. Whatever omelet you can fix up which comes with catsup and will overlap the plate - be sure to put some vegetables in it - but nothing spicy. And another plate of French toast with another of sausage ought to do it. Oh, and a large glass of freshly squeezed orange juice for Duane. He loves it. And hot coffee."

"I'll be right back," Peter assured him.

"Peter!" Carmella hissed, once Peter had cleared the partition. "I think that's them!"

"Yeah, I think so too, Carmella," Peter said, nodding his head. He really needed to calm Carmella. "Don't look so scared, darlin'." he smiled, as he gripped both of Carmella's shoulders. "This is our ship just comin' in!"

Carmella thought about wilting. She would have loved to have wilted right there, into the arms of a brave, resourceful man, who could be counted upon to chart a solution out of any difficulty, but she only had Peter. And if they had any possibility of making this work, Carmella was going to have to be the resolute one. Peter could manage the glad handing. Oh, he was fine up front! But if she didn't hold the center up, if she didn't present a strong armature, she knew he would crumble. She began having visions of that dirt grave off the forest road again.

"That's right, I suppose," Carmella said, forcing a smile and giving Peter a little punch in the shoulder. "Now go out there and be our 'Mayor'."

Peter smiled. He turned. That's what he needed to hear.

As he walked back out with the coffee and juice to meet with his future business associate, a thought flickered across Peter's mind that Carmella was possibly a little bit better woman than he deserved, or at least pretty much so lately, except for a few demerits for bedding that 'serial killer' maniac.

Peter shook his head slightly to clear it of that thought and strode on.

Benny and Peter Talk Shop

Peter re-entered the restaurant proper and placed a large orange juice before Duane and a coffee carafe on the table. He reached behind the counter selecting two cups and set each on the table. "I'm guessing that you might be Mr. Benny Green," Pete said.

"That's me," Benny said.

"Sugar or cream?"

"Both," Benny replied.

Pete passed Benny the cream and sugar and then poured Benny's coffee from the carafe. Then he poured some for himself. "I'm Peter Barnett, Mayor, and owner of this establishment," Peter said, seating himself. "It's good to see you."

"Likewise," Benny said, appraising Peter. "My information is that you are a man of many hats."

"I guess that's true," Pete exclaimed, as if he'd just realized that himself.

"I like hats. I don't wear them myself. But I like them," Benny said.

Peter nodded, not having a clue what this gangster could've meant by that.

"This is my nephew Duane."

"How do you do, Duane."

Duane took no notice but continued slurping his orange juice.

"He gets kind of focused like that." Benny waved his hand.

Peter nodded, and wrapped his hands around his coffee again.

"So. What's the deal with that black spot across the street?" Benny laughed lightly and nodded towards the front window.

"Gas leak." Peter nodded.

Benny nodded.

"So where's the Sheriff? He go up with it?"

"Oh! No. No, he's fine. He's out back actually, using one of our little cabins for an office temporarily." Peter nodded.

Benny nodded. "He'll probably be happy to hear the new

plans?"

"I'd expect so!" Peter smiled. Inside, he wondered.

Benny smiled. Then he dropped his voice. "Look. This is how it is…" Benny paused a moment. "Do you eat first out here?" he asked. "Or you do business first? How does that go? Because I want to do things the way you people do things out here as we start off? You know, so we're all in sync?"

"Either way is fine." Peter raised his coffee to take a sip. "Anyway you want to go."

"Okay, then. Good." Benny dropped his voice. "I've got 5 mil in bills out in the trunk of that car…"

Peter dropped his coffee.

"Shit, man." Benny raised up his stained hands.

"Oh sorry! Sorry!" Peter apologized profusely. He started wiping Benny's hands with this tie. Carmella ran out with a rag.

Peter jerked his head, and Carmella walked away.

"You caught me a little by surprise there," Peter said, glancing out at where he imagined the car.

"Don't look at the car."

"Okay. Sure," Peter said, not thinking, but still trying to look for the car.

"Don't look at the car!"

"Oh! Sorry!" Peter snapped his head back around.

"Jeeeeze." Benny was starting to rub his temples.

"You are green as grass, aren't you," Benny said finally.

"If you mean, have I done this… sort of thing… before? That would be, 'no'." Peter betrayed some nervousness.

"Yeah." Benny nodded.

"Look," Benny said finally. "You want this thing to succeed. And I want this thing to succeed. So from what I can see, right from the gitgo we have no problems! You handle your end of things, and I'll fill you in on my end of things… things should go fine."

Peter nodded rapidly.

"Don't nod so rapidly. It's like a major tell."

Peter looked confused.

"It shows you're nervous!"

Peter nodded slowly.

"Good. So this is how it will work. I'm going to send out a team of people. They will tell you what needs to be done. You will do it."

"What sort of things would that be?" Peter asked hesitantly.

"Does it matter?"

"Uhhh… I'm guessing, "No?" Peter gave him a weak smile.

"You catch on quick. This is good. Don't worry, we don't pat people on the cheek no more. That's just the movies."

Peter blinked.

"But to set your mind at ease, it will just be normal things. We will need to purchase some land - at a good price. We will need the proper zoning. We will need roads and power and sewer and all that. Just normal city affairs I wouldn't think you would have any trouble arranging."

"Uh… okay."

"And I want you to handle the money."

"…handle the money."

"It's a position of much responsibility."

Peter was blinking quite rapidly by then. "Alright..."

"I need you to put this money someplace safe, which you can get to frequently to dole the money out. And not the freezer! Fer Chrissakes," Benny swore, leaning in. "Take you a day to thaw it out, get it to room temperature. Otherwise a moron could tell you where you're keeping it. Got that?"

Peter nodded.

"These people of mine will come to you with 'suggestions'. You will carry them out using this money. And don't misplace a cent, I'm sure I don't have to tell you! I'm fairly forgiving, but my backer in Reno… not so much. There's a lot of desert down there, and he just keeps pouring subdivision after subdivision. Calm down! That's just a joke. " Bennie shook his head. "So just. Don't. Lose the money! Okay?"

"Yeah. Sure! Mr. Benny. I mean, Mr. Green. I read you loud and clear." Peter's left eyelid twitched.

Benny appraised him.

Peter itched his nose. "What if, someone should steal it? I mean, it's a lot of money…"

"That's why you're going to hide it. Real. Good." Benny's forefinger stuck Peter several times in the chest.

Peter sighed, then quickly nodded.

"I got a specialist in money laundering. He'll show you how to pay all of the contractors and arrange for all of the materials with cash. Some people see a construction site and smell the fresh earth? I smell a real money laundering opportunity!" Benny laughed, then just as quickly grew serious.

"And he can assist the contractors too, assuming some to be a little green. The payoffs will be no problem. Those are strictly cash transactions. Eventually, though, we're going to need our own bank. And I've got another friend who can help you with establishing that."

"Establishing a bank?"

Benny looked at him as if to ask, 'We have a problem?'

"You've got a lot of friends," Peter acknowledged.

"Yeah. And soon they're gonna be *yours* too. So don't ever forget *us*. That is, you and me!" Benny emphasized this, stabbing Peter with his finger.

Peter was suddenly a little dizzy with all of the demands. He blinked rapidly, three times, and nodded, wiping his face.

The meals arrived.

Benny finished his. Both of them finished their coffee in silence as Duane gobbled and belched. Finally, Benny pushed back and made what Peter would later decide must have been his best attempt at a pep talk.

"Look," Benny said. "I know you're a fuck-up. And you must know it, otherwise how in hell could you have gotten involved in this? Eh?" Benny laughed gregariously. "Guys on my end, we only get involved with two kinds of people: guys like us and fuckups. Am I right?"

Peter guessed that was probably right, realistically.

"Of course I'm right," Benny agreed. "But in this thing you're going to perform like an ace!" Benny smiled. "And you know why?"

Peter guessed the right thing to do would be to shake his head.

"For the same reason those same schmucks at Stalingrad kept charging the Nazi line."

Peter stared blankly.

"Don't you read? 'Cause turning around and running was a sure shot in the head from the Commies." Benny made the figure of a pistol with his hand and fired it into Peter's head, right above his ear.

Peter nodded.

Carmella noted Benny's gesture from the counter where she was working. She reached up with the rag unconsciously to daub a throbbing headache.

"It's fear, my friend; stark, naked, bone crunching, gut churning *fear*. And *that* is going to give you the backbone you're needing." Benny smiled his biggest smile. He patted Peter warmly on the back before leaving and leaned in to say, "You just stay real *scared* of *me*," Benny indicated both himself and Duane, "and we'll be *real* successful."

Ralph Trains 'Chipper'

While Peter sat on the john, following his terrifying chat with Benny Green, Ralph was up in his hillside studio with 'Chipper'.

Ralph had made quite a few strides with 'Chipper', the name he had given his nemesis, the Chipmunk. Whereas Chipper was the far stronger and more directed when it came to head-on assaults upon Ralph's will, Ralph, however, was much the better at deception. Whatever Ralph wanted Chipper to do, he visualized it as a yummy cashew. It had about the same effect as putting a blonde in a bikini in an ad on a billboard. Chipper simply didn't know what a lie was. And, what was even better, 'Chipper' seemed unable to learn.

Chipper would fall for the same misdirection again and again, until the misdirection itself became a kind of second language. It was quite a rudimentary 'language' to be sure, but it allowed Chipper and Ralph to communicate, nevertheless. And from here, a great 'friendship' was born. Harnessed to the Chipmunk's feral regions, Ralph's will became a powerhouse. While harnessed to Ralph's guile the Chipmunk became a small animal intruder of incredible shrewdness and stealth. He could unlock a deadbolt, turn a knob. He could dig through the cupboards until he found the salt. He could get money or a credit card from Ralph's wallet, or find his reading glasses and a pen and paper. He could even fetch the jam or the butter.

They began eating together at the counter. Ralph would tape a little bib or napkin to the Chipmunks chest and serve him his meal in a beer bottle cap. He found that Chipper especially liked his nuts lightly sautéed in an oyster sauce. And that for breakfast he enjoyed a few buttered toast crumbs. He also liked to chew the overcooked edges of Ralph's egg and mushroom frittata and enjoyed munching on mung bean sprouts as between meal snacks.

One evening, Ralph tried sharing a little after dinner beer. He gave Chipper a few capfuls and found himself waking up deep in the forest, that next morning, inside of a rotten log with just a raging headache. So he scuttled that idea.

'Perhaps the meek *shall* inherit the earth,' Ralph thought, as he cast the postman a smile which could devour a steak, as they chatted one day. They were 'chatting' about maybe not making Ralph walk all the way into town to get parcels which were clearly sized properly to fit within Ralph's supersized box.

"Weakness is provocative," would probably be the only explanation the postman, Bill, could have given for his formerly oafish behavior - had he the intelligence to discern it.

But the effect of Ralph's new presence was so daunting, that this rural mail carrier fell backwards, then had to turn himself turtle to right himself before standing.

When the mail carrier stopped for coffee at the Campaign Café, he couldn't help remarking across the counter what a change had overtaken "that crazy, stumblebum of a poet/painter, who lives up the ridge. He had a… I don't know what else to call it, but a…. way about him that scared the shit outta *me!* The rural postman declared to all at the counter. *"I told him, Fine. You want it in the box, you got it inside the box. I wasn't going to argue the matter, I can tell you that! Plus, he up and pushed me."* The latter accusation dribbled off in a manner that told all within earshot that this latter much of it, at least, was a lie.

None of the other farmers at the counter thought that much of it. Nobody gave Bill Parsons much credibility. He was known not to deliver a letter if he found the stamp attached sideways. And they hemmed and hawed at the counter that morning, not granting Bill much traction, mostly just turning their attention away, ostensibly to cough.

Nevertheless, when Bill walked around behind to deliver the mail to the Sheriff immediately following his coffee, he made it a point to *"put a bug into the Sheriff's ear, too"*.

Bill Porter, the Mailman, Runs to the Sheriff

The sunlight through the bare window made the top of Leland's desk hot and was making his left arm sweat, as he pushed the pen around some more. A few more signatures and he was done. He heard an insect buzzing around the windowsill. He was pushing himself back from the desk, when Agent Perez appeared, first as a silhouette in the doorway, then as a full blown, lit swarthy figure in a dark suit.

"Where are my people?" Leland demanded.

Agent Perez took a moment to take Leland's measure before answering. "Right now, we still don't know."

Leland spared a moment to consider Agent Perez' response, then nodded.

"I thought I'd drop past and see how you were doing." Agent Perez stood squarely in the center of the small office, hands on hips, like a Colossus thigh deep in the Mediterranean.

"Whoever blew up my office caused me a lot of paperwork." Leland eyeballed Agent Perez.

Agent Perez walked over to gaze out the window. A tattoo of the head of a snake just peaked over the collar of Agent Perez' dress shirt as his head turned. Red blood dripped from its teeth. "Well, he's out there somewhere. Probably surviving on roots and berries, huh? That should make you feel a little better."

"That, or he's got a gun to some farmer's head as his wife fixes him a nice meal with a big slice of apple pie."

Agent Perez nodded. "Well, no one really knows for sure, do we?" Agent Perez eyed Leland. "We'll get him. We've got eyes in the sky. We've got agents on the ground."

"You know, I was going to talk to you about that. I'd be a little more comfortable if you'd introduce me to these agents you have walking around. It's always good to be able to pick out the good guys from the bad, if things come to that."

Perez nodded as he craned his neck to peer further out the window. "If it comes to that, I'll let you know. Looks like the mail might be here!"

Sure enough, Bill Parsons was steaming up the yard towards Leland's cottage office.

Perez fetched himself a chair. They waited. Bill knocked timidly on the door frame. Leland waited. Bill knocked harder on the door frame. "Come in!" Leland waited.

Finally, a red faced Bill Porter appeared in the doorway, and exclaimed, in a big rush of wind, "I've been pushed!"

Sheriff Leland looked sympathetic. "Are you okay?"

"Well, yeah." Bill Porter paused to consider, still a bit dizzy from the two cold beers he'd just had, then his countenance screwed up with indignation again. "It's that crazy Ralph Bunch the artist, or poet, or whateverheis. He wanted me to hand him a parcel that it was clearly against regulations to deliver to him there, and that he needed to come down to the post office to get. Which is why I brought it all the way up there to show him!" Bill included Agent Perez in his indignation but sensing no good will there at all, turned back to Leland. "And then, well, he smiled a smile like I've never seen on him before... and then, he must have pushed me!"

"*Must* have pushed you?"

"Well. It knocked me onto my back..."

"What knocked you onto your back?"

Bill looked at a loss for words. "I don't know. I guess it must have been his *smile*."

Agent Perez guffawed at this. Leland cast Perez a dark look. Bill considered, then straightened. "All I know is that Ramey is looking and acting really strange way out there in the woods and all, and I think you ought to go out and have a talk with him. There. That's it."

"That sounds like a good idea to me Bill. And I will see if I can't get out there as soon as possible."

"Well. That's it, then. That's all I wanted to say, I guess." Bill

Porter shrugged.

"I appreciate you taking the time to stop by, Bill. As our postman you are the eyes and ears to a lot of what's happening around here, and it would be hard to police this county as well as we have without your willingness to share."

Bill glowed a bit. "Well, okay. Thanks Sheriff. I guess, I'd better get on to my rounds now."

"Okay." Leland waved. "We'll see you."

Bill Porter exited.

"Jesus, the way you suck up to these mindless yokels," Agent Perez said.

Eldon Cene

The Big Colt Anaconda

After Bill Parsons, the mailman, had made his exit, Leland rose and walked to the door. He looked outside. It was a lovely, hot summer day. A few cotton candy cumuli floated in the sky. Leland stared at them a while and listened to the noontime sounds of his small town. He could hear the fry cook yelling through the back door of the Campaign Café about a half block away. A kid rode past on his bike with a card in the spokes. It made sounds like crickets. He was hoping he had a little longer on this earth. Then he took a deep breath and shut the door behind him.

When Leland was resettled at his desk, Perez spoke. "I think you know where your crew is," he said.

Leland nodded. But whether it was to acknowledge that he had heard Perez, or that he agreed, Agent Perez couldn't tell.

"First off, because you have a local's knowledge of the area and wherever it is they might be hiding themselves - for whatever reason they *might* be hiding themselves. Which I have to add, escapes me. Unless our fugitive is holding them hostage, which conflicts with my next reason." Agent Perez leaned forward a bit. "Which is second, because I just haven't noticed that much concern upon your part in finding them. You don't just fill out insurance forms, I'm thinking. You also do detective work? That is, police work? Right?"

Leland said nothing, as if weighing what Perez had said. Then he slowly wheeled his office chair back a foot and opened the desk drawer. His big Colt Anaconda was the first object to appear. And Leland noted out of the corner of his eye, Agent Perez' right hand jumped just perceptibly towards his left side, then slackened as Leland's hand reached further into the drawer. He brought out a slim manila envelope which he tossed across the desktop to Agent Perez. "You ever seen this fellow?" He asked.

Agent Perez slowly withdrew the page-sized glossy photo of himself. His shock was apparent, though he struggled to hide it. He

68

mustered a thin smile. "Where did you get this?"

"Oh. It was something which came up during the course of our *police work*." Leland nodded.

"Well." Agent Perez admired the photo. "I have to say, I like the photographer. He makes me look years younger."

"You *were* years younger." Leland nodded.

"There you go," Perez said, tossing the photo back onto the desktop. "At one time, I *was* much younger." He rested both palms on his thighs. They both sat like two gunfighters, wondering whose move would be next.

Leland leaned slightly forward. "Do you know where that was taken? Pinch, West Virginia."

"No shit? Well, imagine that. I'll bet *most* people couldn't even find Pinch, West Virginia on a map."

"Only three that I know of."

"Yeah?"

"Yeah. Two of whom have lost their heads." Leland nodded. "Pick up that photo and look at it again."

Agent Perez' brows compressed in a puzzled expression, but he complied, picking up the photo again with his right hand.

Leland had the big Colt Anaconda in his hand and aimed, before Perez dropped the photo to reach for his own.

"No. No, that's good. Just continue reaching into your left side holster there and hand me your weapon, real slow, by the butt. I'm sure you know the drill." Leland directed.

Agent Perez shook his head.

Leland took the gun butt with his left hand and ejected the clip. He put the clip in the lowest drawer and the gun in the next lowest. Then he shut and locked both drawers.

"Agent Perez," Leland said. "We need to talk."

"I Can't Tell You How Important Aliens are to Our Work"

"I'm glad to hear you say that," Agent Perez said with a hollow laugh. "'Cause for a moment there, I thought you were going to shoot me. You want me to put my hands up, or something?"

"If you'd like," Leland said.

Perez laughed. "There's really no need for this. We're really on the same side here."

"Okay." Leland nodded. "I'd like to hear you tell me about that."

Perez nodded.

"Look," Perez said. "We're both on the same page here. We both want that lunatic Stan, as he calls himself, taken out. I mean, he's already cut the heads off two women from just around here, and then killed a farm couple. Am I right?"

"I'm listening."

"So what it is, is I'm thinking that somehow or other he's got to you. He's convinced you somehow, that I'm acting in an adversarial way towards you - or might be. Which is why, I can't locate either him or your crew, because I think you have him tied up somewhere and are just so spooked by this whole affair that you've figured the best thing to do is to go to ground until the situation clarifies. I mean, if I were a small town Sheriff with all of your meager resources, and I thought there was something going on here that might involve 'higher government agencies', as Stan has it visualized in his operated on, Post Traumatic Stress Syndromes, already compromised cranium - then I might do the very same thing." His brows rose. He nodded. "But you know, threatening a Federal employee with a firearm is a highly punishable offence."

Leland held up his palm to stop him there. With his left hand he drew out a drawer from the left side and laid it on the desktop. Then he rested his gun hand on that.

"This damned thing gets heavy," Leland remarked.

Perez shook his head.

Leland raised the tip of the gun, indicating that Perez should continue. Which Perez did.

"So, as I was saying, pointing a weapon, especially one large as that, at a federal officer is a highly criminal act."

"It's my understanding that they usually drop the lesser charges."

Perez frowned.

"But I've been frank with you!" There was a note of pleading in Perez' voice. "This case *does* involve higher government agencies. But I've told you that just by being here, right? It's not like our perp, Stan, has given you any hard knowledge. The first time we met, didn't I give show you all my identification and all that?"

Leland reached into the drawer and brought out a faxed page, which he dropped on the desktop on top of the photo.

Perez crunched his brows and then inspected it. He smacked it with the back of his hand. "You see! Here it is. Official confirmation of my status." He looked further. "Signed, by one of your own." He offered it back to Leland.

Leland tossed it into the trash.

"It's a little habit that my friend has. He likes embossed paper. Always does his work on embossed paper. Comes from a family of blue bloods. It was a joke between us that his family crest was on everything he created." Leland offered the trash can to Perez.

Perez didn't bother. Instead he just shook his head and exhaled.

"One of those days, huh?" Leland commiserated, setting the can.

Perez nodded. He made as if to reach for his vest pocket.

"It okay if I smoke?"

"If you stand up slowly, take off your jacket, turn once with your arms outstretched and then toss the jacket to me."

Perez nodded and did so. "The smokes are in the lower right corner pocket."

Leland dug them out and handed them to him along with the

matches. Perez nodded his thanks and lit up. He inhaled gratefully.

"Okay. Obviously my cover is blown wide open." He puffed on his cigarette. "I just can't believe that maniac is making me look like the bad buy here, but here goes." He took another couple puffs. "My real name is, Agent Louis."

"Oh. So it's just the surnames which are different." Leland shook his head.

"This is tough enough without some no account Podunk town Sheriff having to be a wise ass, okay?"

Leland raised a brow.

"Sorry. Sorry. What I *meant* is, that I'm on top of a whole slab of shit which is slowly, slowly, and then more rapidly shifting sideways, and I've yet to get a handle on it. And this should concern you, too. Because if everything breaks loose as I'm afraid it might, then this Stan maniac is going to be the least of our worries. That is, yours and mine."

"I think it's broken loose, at least for you." Leland smiled grimly. "But go ahead. You were saying..."

"You're right. This whole thing had its... *latest* origins back in Pinch, West Virginia in October of 1986. A busload of schoolgirls on their way to a debate tournament had disappeared for 6 hours and my unit was dispatched to find out what was going on."

"Your unit?"

"I'm a fixer. I do clean-up."

"Who do you work for?"

"Nobody."

Leland cocked the hammer of the gun.

"I'm not lying. I'm serious! We're all *nobodies*. We don't exist. Stan is a nobody. *He* doesn't exist. All of these operations that are going on - *none of them exist.* It's all done so that no one can trace either the monies or the identities. Currently we organize our activities through Twitter."

"You 'tweet' each other."

"That's about the gist of it." Perez nodded. "We all are

employed under different names and different government sectors, we just don't work there. We work here. As far anyone knows, I am working for the Federal Bureau of Fisheries. At least that's what my benefits statement says."

"You like your job?

Perez rolled his eyes. "It's okay."

Leland nodded.

"Ever so often I have to go out on a boat, which I don't like so much. I get seasick real easy. But the accountants run the placement. We haven't much say about that."

Leland nodded again. Perez took another drag. He shook his head and sighed.

"Somewhere, in some very deep, blacked out hole in the bowels of somewhere - who knows, maybe the Postal Service, but of course, it didn't have anything to do with the Postal Service - they were doing experiments I was told on the "Mind/Body Connection".

"Some kind of yoga thing?"

"Ha! If only. We'd both have out little sponge mats rolled up under our arms and heading over to the 'hot yoga' studio. No. These sci-fi nerds were trying to disconnect the mind/body connection. It all has something to do with computer theory. As it was explained to me, the geniuses that run these experiments theorized that human thought was basically an algorithm which is 'substrate independent' from the brain, just like the relationship of any computational device with its software. So just as a person can build a simple computer out of just about anything you can arrange into open and closed gates, ones and zeroes, so to should a mind be capable of utilizing other substrates to perform its functions. The feeling was that the human brain, as a substrate for mind work, had just about maxed out. We needed a better substrate, and the evolutionary process was moving us way to slow. The machines are getting ahead of us.

"Machines are getting ahead of us?" Leland repeated.

Perez nodded. "So if they were to create a super-intelligent race they would have to find a better substrate for the human mind. Or, perhaps alter the human brain in ways that would increase its computational abilities. Stan was an experiment of this second sort. Nancy Loomis was an experiment of the first sort.

By cutting the workload on certain areas of the brain through surgical intervention, Stan's mind was able to more fully utilize its substrate. This has given him extraordinary speed, but decreased his empathy, as you may have noticed."

"Notice made," Leland replied.

"The young girls, on the other hand, were treated and monitored over a period of several hours with a virus, recovered from the tinctures of one unusual Jamaican voodoo practitioner, which apparently works over a period of from several hours to several years to detach the human mind from its substrate. Have you ever heard of the term "Nightwalkers"?

"No," Leland said.

"These were the zombie like creatures which the Jamaican voodoo practitioners created when their tinctures detached their patient's minds from their bodies. Oftentimes they got into all sorts of troubles, as the mental running apparatus left in the zombie was basically the stem plus amygdaloidal body - in other words they were left in a very atavistic state, like wild men.   So they were often hunted down and killed. But now and then, one of the minds would drift about and find a way to re-attach. In which case, these patients became individuals later capable of leaving their bodies for intervals at a time to drift around. As you can imagine, the military especially became interested in exploring these capabilities. And by 1986 someone felt that they were ready for human trials. "

"I was sent there in October of 1986 just to cushion the girls' re-entry and to keep tabs on the press. There wasn't much to do, really. The bus was clean. No clues to what had occurred. And the girls seemed fine, except for the six hours of amnesia. We just kept our hands off, and eventually the episode was forgotten as just another unexplainable episode of alien abduction for want of a better theory.

I can't tell you how handy aliens are to our work."

Further Interrogation

Agent Perez sat there silently smoking. Apparently he felt that he'd said everything that he needed to say. Leland raised his brows. Perez shrugged.

"You want me to say, I'm sorry?" He asked.

Leland shook his head. "I wouldn't believe it."

"Best not to waste my time then." Perez started to rise.

"Did I tell you, you could move?" Leland asked. "Next time you move, for any reason, I pull this trigger."

Perez sat back down, softly. "What is it you *want* me to say?"

"It's more a matter of what *you want you* to say," Leland corrected him.

Agent Perez looked puzzled.

"What *more* can you think of to say, that will get you out of here alive?" Leland put it to him more plainly.

"I can't think of anything."

"Then your chances don't look very good."

"You're nuts! You know that?" Agent Perez broke the long, silent stand-off.

Leland almost hated to hear him do it. He had been enjoying the hot, silent sound of the noonday downtown Kimmel, save for a few crickets and a logging rig or two passing through. He'd been wondering how Agent Hailey was doing with the rest of them holed up at the dentist's. He was wondering how the reporter girl could stay away from home or school as long as she remained missing and not cause any concern. He was wondering how Ramey, the dentist, was getting along with Nancy Loomis, the disembodied intelligence. He figured that Merlin Travers, his friend the vet, was probably back at his own workplace by now as his sort of business couldn't be put off. He wondered about had gotten into Ralph Bunch of late. And Leland was just up to considering giving Merlin a call when Agent Perez broke the spell. "I'm sorry," Leland said. "I was considering something. What is it you were saying?"

"You're a little off your nut, that's what I was saying!" Perez shouted. "In fact," he noted grimly, "I'm wondering if maybe it wasn't *you* who killed those two agents of ours who've gone missing. Maybe Stan didn't have anything to do with that one at all. Seeing as you are so fast and loose with the firepower."

"Hmmmmm." Leland nodded, considering. "From your side of things I'd guess it wouldn't seem that out of character."

"Yeah, doesn't it? Trigger happy small town Sheriff kills two government employees, by mistake. A definitely could've happened. Then, tries to pin it on our serial killer!"

"Why would I want to kill 'two government employees'?" Leland asked with interest. "And if two federal employees are dead, why haven't we heard of it?"

"Because they were sent here to look around and find Stan and pull him out. And then, they disappeared."

"Okay."

"When people like us *disappear*, you don't hear anything," Perez explained, with extreme patience.

"That *is* good to know." Leland nodded.

Perez looked at the gun.

"When people like *myself* die, we would appear to go out with a big boom!" Leland shifted the big gun grimly.

"That wasn't me. That was a call from way above my pay grade. We had a rouge agent who was not only killing no-longer sanctioned civilians, but our own agents besides. He had to go. He had to be taken out, and as quickly and as certainly as was possible. Sometimes, there's collateral damage." Perez held his palms up and shrugged. "You want me to say, I'm sorry?"

"Nope. We covered that."

"Well, there it is then." Perez patted his thighs. "It turned out alright anyway, as far as I can see. You obviously got all of your people out safely and have our prisoner in custody. So it's a win-win. You give the guy to us. We disappear. All is back to normal."

"You blew up my Sheriff's office. Two farmers around here are dead now because of you."

Perez corrected him. "Because of Stan, a serial killer."

"Who you engineered..."

Perez shook his head. "I don't engineer anything. As I've said before, I'm a *'fixer'*. I *fix* things. We're on the same side here. And when I go away, all of your troubles go away."

"I've got to say, you paint a compelling case."

"Good. I thought you'd see reason eventually. Now, I've got to go," Perez said, rising.

Leland shot him through the heart. "I *told* you not to move."

The gun was heavy enough that the kick wasn't all that bad.

The bullet left an inch-sized hole in Agent Perez' chest. The impact of it slid both Perez and the chair into the far wall, where Perez looked calm as could be with a half-opened mouth - as if about to add something. Blood was puddling on the floor. There was quite a bit of splatter.

Leland observed his work while reflecting on something his partner on the police force had once said: "Things start to sort themselves out - after you've killed some people." Leland certainly hoped so.

Leland holstered the heavy gun, figuring now would be a good time to finish making that call to Merlin.

A Very Good Friend

"You see?" Merlin exclaimed, examining the carnage. "This is why I'm not a big fan of guns."

Leland admitted to himself that seeing it could be a shock. Perez was stuck there, against the wall in the clotted blood, with his mouth open as if to frame his next words and his eyes riveted on something which was no longer a thought.

"You give a fellow a big gun," Merlin waved at Leland, "and there's just no way that sooner or later, somehow or other, he's not going to find a way to use it!" Merlin stomped about and pissed and moaned.

Leland let him vent for a while. After all, Leland knew he was asking Merlin for quite a bit. It's hard to be asked to travel from veterinarian and small and large animals one moment, to accessory to murder the next. And even harder to do it. And for that Leland had to give Merlin a pat on the back.

"I'll admit, that on the face of it, that might appear to be what happened. But Merlin, I really feel that this all serves a greater good," Leland gave Merlin a couple good man-sized pats with a comrade's rub tossed in.

Merlin sighed. He tossed up his arms again and sat.

They both sat watching the body cool. Leland finally broke out the bottle of Three Feathers. Then they sat watching a while longer, while the body cooled and stiffened and began to blanch.

"I've got to say that when I kept harping on you to reduce the size of government, this wasn't exactly what I had in mind," Merlin said finally, waving at Perez.

"Yeah..." Leland said, setting his drink and getting out of his chair to lift the body.

Merlin shook his head, as he patted his knees and rose. "Yeah. Yup. On the other hand... You want me to help you lift?"

"If you would?" Leland grunted.

Eldon Cene

Feeding the Hogs

"One. Two. Three!"

Agent Perez (RIP) landed with a *thud* and a little splatter in the muck, about a yard inside the hog pen where he stuck.

"Maybe we oughta have removed the body bag," Leland second guessed himself, when he saw the Weed's hogs were slow to examine their dinner.

"No. We left a good crack in the zippered sack. They've probably just been fed. I'll tell Bill Porter to leave off feeding them because I'll be looking in on them for a few days. Tomorrow morning they'll wake up hungry and make short work of this 'Dark Op'. And if they don't eat the sack, I'll run a few of the goats in there. Make for a nice clean crime scene." Merlin turned away, then turned back fingering his car keys. "You want to say anything, before we go?"

"Say anything? What do you mean? About what?"

Merlin shook his head and looked down.

"Oh," Leland said. "Oh! Of course. You know I figured it went without saying, that I really appreciate your help on this Merlin." But this wasn't what Merlin had meant.

Merlin stole a glance at the corpse of Agent Perez in the black body bag.

"You mean... like last words? Commend his soul to God?"

"Something like that, I suppose." Merlin nodded.

Leland glanced at the sky.

"I'm sorry. But I really can't recommend him," Leland said. He fingered the agent's wallet and identification he had kept in his jacket pocket.

Merlin shook his head and showed his disappointment.

"What?" Leland asked. "What?"

"You know what's wrong with you, Leland?"

"From the look you're giving me, I'd guess, probably not."

"Pride."

"Pride?"

"Pride. You don't see anything about that guy we just dumped in the muck that resembles yourself in the least," Merlin noted. "And so you have no sympathy."

"Merlin. If you didn't want to help me do this, you should've just said so. Because now is not a good time to start with the recriminations, deconstruction of, and nasty remarks about… my character."

"When would be a good time?"

Leland thought about this. "You really expect me to answer that?"

Merlin looked at him.

"How about never? Would NEVER work for you?"

Merlin keep staring.

"Okay, fine." Leland put out his hand for the keys. "How about on the ride back? Would on the ride back work for you? Maybe once we pass the three mile perimeter."

Merlin tossed the keys to Leland.

Leland Explains It All to Merlin

If he hadn't crossed the three mile perimeter yet, it didn't matter, because by the looks of Merlin, it was time for Leland to speak. Besides, that was the least Leland could do seeing as how Merlin had been sticking his neck out pretty far for Leland of late.

"Okay. How does this go now? Do I just cop a plea and apologize for my character defects as you itemize them? Or do I defend myself vigorously?"

Merlin stared ahead down the highway.

"Or is this one of those Freudian things where you don't say a word while I lie back in the driver's seat and talk until it finally all gets down to my mother?" Leland sighed.

"I don't want to hear about your mother."

"Alright. Good! We can start from there." The road shot past as Leland beat the steering wheel.

"Okay. I shot a guy. Point made. And I don't feel bad about it. Point made, again." Leland nodded. He noticed he had let the speedometer climb up into the 80s and Merlin was looking a little concerned. He slowed the car.

"He's a human being, Leland. And we just tossed him to the hogs."

"A lot nicer end than being buried and slowly rotting away with bugs and maggots and worms drilling in and out, to my way of thinking." The car slowed to 55 where Leland put it on cruise control.

"So we did a good thing?"

"Well, yeah, more or less. Time will tell, I suppose." Leland thought about this. "Look Merlin, you're not in law enforcement so you may not have had a reason to learn this. But when you decide you have to do a hard thing - there's no point in feeling bad about it. There's no upside to that. All you want to feel is pleased, that it came off successful. I mean, that could have been me back there. Did you notice that the man was carrying?"

"His holster was empty."

"That's 'cause I took it. I've got all his ID and his weapon, plus I grabbed his prints and did a DNA kit before you arrived. When I went for my gun, he went for his. I won."

They had been going a regular speed long enough now that Merlin felt it safe to turn towards Leland to speak. "It doesn't feel right to kill a guy and feed him to the hogs, and then not even say something."

"Well. That's what I'm doing. I'm saying something."

"I haven't heard a word of remorse yet."

"And you're not going to. What I'm saying is something different."

"It sure is. Very different." Merlin sighed finally. Merlin indicated with his finger that Leland should look at the road now. Leland looked and jerked the wheel a bit to take them back into their lane. "Okay. What is it? What is it that you have to say for yourself that's *different?*"

Leland considered. "You ever try to talk to a teenager about something they've done, Merlin?" He finally asked.

Merlin waved his head and shook his hands. "Like about what? What are we talking about?!"

"Talking to teenagers."

"Uh, jeeze."

"Take a deep breath, Merlin. And I will reward your patience."

"That would be an awfully big reward."

"Then maybe take a really deep breath," Leland advised.

"One of the things that makes it so hard to reason with a teenager is that you're not really talking to them." To assuage Merlin, Leland made a big event of taking a *good* look at the road before he launched into it.

The scenery never changed around here, he thought. Off to the left were evergreens. Off to the right were evergreens. Blackberry brambles filled in the gaps nearest the roadside. Further in were ferns and moss, toppled trees, cut stumps and mushrooms. It was like they were living on a big sponge where most of the year it rained except for now. Summers were nice. Leland got to meditating on this, then realized he needed to continue talking to his friend.

"You're really talking to all of their friends, or to people who they aspire to be their friends and trying to reason with *them*." Leland's brows rose. "Only they are not there. Only the teenager is there. So you can't really get at the minds of the people you really have to change in order to change this particular teenager's mind. Because they don't answer to you." Leland glanced back at the road. A logging truck passed tooting his horn. Leland honked. Leland eyed Merlin, to see if he were making any headway.

"So. There isn't much to be done except shoot them," Merlin observed.

"Don't think parents haven't considered this." Leland nodded.

Leland raised a cautioning hand. They were passing the cutoff to the Jamison's old homestead road. "Just follow me for a moment, here. One of the reasons teenagers get into so much trouble is that they are responding to what they 'fear' their peer group demands. So rather than to just show that they can drink; they have to drink themselves blotto. Rather than to just have a girlfriend, they have to brag about some great sexual conquest. In their head, their *fears* won't allow them a rational, measured response - because the penalties of falling short are just too great, it would seem, to them."

'There, that ought to do it,' Leland thought. He watched and they were passing the Cook's farmstead on the right. Nothing looked amiss.

"This is real handy to know, Leland. And I'm going to make a note of it as soon as I get back to the office." Merlin nearly spit. "You just killed a guy, Leland. Why? Why?!! That's really all I want to know - and think I deserve to know."

Leland nodded.

"You do. And you do. And I'm getting to that, right now."

"Good."

"This guy was reacting hysterically."

Leland nodded as the Cliffords and the Wentz's moved past.

"He didn't look hysterical. In fact, he looked real calm… stuck to the wall, maybe, but real *calm*."

Then the Moran's on the right moved past. Leland realized tardily, as always, that he had to cinch up this thinking better. Paint a fuller picture. Put in all the cows. It wasn't enough to say you saw a barn and smelled the manure.

"We started out with two decapitated women." Leland raised two fingers. "And now, at present count we have seven dead, a van load of injured Japanese tourists and one obliterated Sheriff's office. This is not making things go away. This is causing something to make the national news. Whoever was running this guy panicked! And there would never be enough deaths to put whoever that is, totally at ease. And he will never be totally at ease, because whoever this is, is not calling the shots. Instead, he is anticipating what whoever it is who would be calling the shots would do to *him*, if, whoever that is decides he had to step in and call some shots. Which, to my thinking, would *not* bode too well for whoever it is who is running our friend there in the hog's pen."

"Okay. I think I follow." Merlin shook his head sarcastically, indicated that he felt he was on a fool's errand. "But why won't they just send in more guys, to do what the first wave failed to accomplish… that is, to kill all of us?"

"Because," Leland nodded, "I am now a murderer, too."

Merlin evaluated his friend.

They were back in the trees, back in the land of the endless evergreens on both sides.

"I just made my bones. So. Now I am one of them. Who better to have on their roster but the local law? They don't have to kill anyone anymore, because now it's all on my head to keep everything quiet." Leland scrutinized the walls over evergreens they passed.

A sober Merlin evaluated his friend and noticed what he hadn't noticed before - that is, that he was slumped.

Back at Ramey's

"All we have to do now is to hope they realize this," Leland continued, once they'd reached Ramey's to address the others.

Ramey's appeared much as they'd left it. No outward signs of habitation. Cars left in the shed. Blinds drawn. They walked around back and gave the 'tap' and the door was opened by Agent Hailey with her piece drawn.

"Well, Agent Perez is dead," Leland told them.

"Who's Agent Perez?" They all asked.

So Leland told them.

"Oh, that's the smart move!" Stan said sarcastically. "Why hadn't I thought of that? We just climb the ladder killing them one by one." He turned to Merlin. "How many people was it you say work for the government?"

"How did Agent Perez die?" Agent Hailey asked.

"Of old age," Stan replied. "He got as old as he was going to get." Stan eyeballed Leland. "The Sheriff here shot him. Am I right?"

"He's dead," Leland replied.

Stan nodded. Agent Hailey looked horrified.

"Don't worry," Merlin said. "We disposed of the body well."

Nancy Gillis took out her pencil and pad and began writing. Ruth looked very worried. Ramey was napping. And Agent Hailey had to sit.

"You just up and shot him?" Agent Hailey declared, looking up.

"Pretty much." Leland nodded.

"Well, we're dead." Stan sighed. "These people are bigger than the mob. These people could be anyone throughout the entire government. They could even be me, or you, or you, or you..." Stan indicated Ruth, Merlin, Agent Hailey. "Or even you." Stan indicated Nancy Gillis.

"Not me," said Nancy.

"Why not you?" asked Stan.

"'Cause I'm only fifteen."

Stan laughed. "You people!" His head shook. "You are so *naïve*."

"And you are so mentally… compromised," Ruth retorted.

Benny Comes to Call

Leland left them all arguing. He pointed to their stole-away student reporter, Nancy Gillis, as he exited. "Merlin, keep your eye on her."

"If I have to, I'll stuff her in a dog kennel," Merlin assured him.

Leland intended to set up a meeting with whoever ran Agent Perez at the Café. But before he did so, Leland wanted to check on Ralph Bunch. But before that he had to return to the office to do a little clean-up.

The fresh paint was just drying when Benny stuck his head in the door.

He looked around. "Well, it's small but inadequate." Benny laughed.

Leland looked up from the brush he was cleaning. "And you are…?"

"I'm Green. Benny Green." Benny stepped forward to offer Leland his hand. But Leland begged off, indicating with a nod how he was fairly up to his ears in the paint.

"What can I do for you, Mr. Green?" Leland asked.

Leland was very interested in what Benny Green might want here in Kimmel. He remembered what Agent Hailey's colleague, Agent Curtis, had said, and he had discarded the theory. But this appearance of Mr. Green - in the flesh - was interesting.

"We share a mutual friend," Benny said.

"I suppose we do," Leland answered, amused that Agent Curtis was Benny's idea of a friend.

"Pete, the Mayor, said that you were fairly low key," Benny glanced around, "but managed to do an effective job on what amounts to a very low budget." Benny nodded approvingly. "I like that."

"Oh, so you know Peter Barnett also." Leland finished his chores.

"I thought that's what I'd said."

"Yeah," Leland straightened. "I suppose you did."

Leland indicated the coffee service, then finished cleaning his hands and picking up.

Benny selected one of the porcelain mugs brought over from the café, searched for the cream and sugar and found none. "There's no cream and sugar."

"Nope."

"You must not get any visitors." Benny held up his palms. "No, no, I understand. Your place of business blows up? People are reluctant to re-frequent. It's happened to me, many times. Don't worry about it. Things'll get back to normal." Benny took a sip, as he settled his one haunch on the edge of the Sheriff's desk. "You find out who done it?"

Leland stood up and stretched. "It was a gas leak."

"According to Pete, this town isn't plumbed for gas."

"Well, he's the mayor. He ought to know."

"It sounds though like your offices *were* 'plumbed for gas', in a manner of speaking."

"That's more than likely accurate." Leland nodded.

"So who did that?" Benny asked.

"What can I do for you Mr. Green?" Leland answered.

"I'm thinking Peter hasn't spoken to you much about him and me?" Benny said. "You know, our partnership with the city and impending plans for the Kimmel area?"

"My specialty is crime. So unless it's a crime, the mayor doesn't usually include me in his circle of confidants. And if it is crime?" Leland gave Benny Green a steady glance. "Then it is my job to *find*, pursue, arrest and to charge it."

Benny pursued his lips and nodded.

"Are you planning any crime here in Kimmel?" Leland asked, while he seated himself.

"Well," Benny considered thoughtfully. "Maybe?"

"Then we might still have a problem. You see this is still all Kimmel county. And I'm the Kimmel county Sheriff. What are you here looking for? Maybe to sign up for a 'Crime Permit'?"

"Hmmmm. I'd never heard it put quite that way, but maybe. How much are they?"

Leland opened the desk drawer and pulled out a clipboard with some auto impound form on it. "What crime is it you would wish to commit?" He smiled. "Dollar volume? The number of Sheriff's staff involved? And then of course we need some background. Have you ever committed a crime before? Successful? Unsuccessful? What is your record with the law? Have you ever undertaken an enterprise of this nature previously? What is your criminal experience? And then, of course, there are the fingerprints, DNA swabbing and blood tests for drugs. We don't allow drugs. And you'd have to take a complete physical exam."

"Would you quit fucking with me? I drove all the way out to this cowpie of a burg to initiate some serious business."

Leland put the clipboard away and pulled out the gun. "Okay," he said. "Let's be serious." He aimed the big Colt Anaconda right at Benny Green's balls.

Benny Green nodded and sat. "Now we're talking," he said.

Benny laid out the situation. And after he'd done that, he said, "There's no reason for me to keep any of this from you, as you would more than likely figure out most of it yourself, some of which you have already, I'd guess," he said, nodding at the gun. "But sometimes, you know, what people tend to think of as 'bad' things can lead to very good results. We bring a large investment to the area, the local economy benefits, employment is good, and we keep things safe. We, in the 'adult recreation business', know how to protect our customers. The streets of Kimmel - the one or two blocks or whatever there are - will be very safe," Benny assured

Leland.

"And what do you expect of me?" Leland asked.

Benny smiled. "We expect you to enjoy your new Sheriff's offices and jail! We'd expect you'd enjoy a hefty raise in pay and the budget to hire several more deputies and staff. We'd expect you to be relieved to have our complete backing when the next election comes around."

Leland put away the gun. "I'm going to have to start offering cream and sugar," he said. "Is there anything else I'd expect?"

"Well, this is not me. This would be my partners expectations…"

Leland nodded.

"But they would expect to call the shots," Benny's brows shot up, apologetically.

"They would be the law."

"More or less," Benny nodded. "But only in special instances! Which, at the moment, I can't foresee. But you probably know how these big time people are. They're alphas. They always insist on calling the shots. That's just the way they are. That's why I'm here, more or less. They don't negotiate well. So I'm their buffer. But if everything goes according to plan, I don't see them ever even appearing. And, if we work well together, we retain the PG Rating. Everybody wins."

Leland nodded. "So, how long do I have to consider this?"

Benny leaned forward and smiled. "How long do you think you have?"

"I'd guess as long as I want - as long as the answer is "Yes"," Leland replied.

"You see!" Benny clapped Leland on the shoulder. "This is why I think we will work well together. I don't have to spell things out for you. Why, we'll be like two hands, the left hand always anticipating what the right is up to. You'll see! This will be a quite successful enterprise."

Leland nodded.

"Which brings up one other thing," Benny said. "I'm concerned about whoever blew up your office. It seems like there is something going on around here, I'm not privy to. And I don't like that. If we become allies, and then someone blows up you - where does that leave me then? Or, what if they decide that since we're allies, they might like to blow me up too? Which I would like even less! So, you want to tell me who you think it is? Perhaps, as a first test of our partnership, I can look into it and perhaps dissuade them for you."

Leland shook his head. "Nice of you to offer, Benny." Leland stood. "But I'm preparing to handle that next and hope to have the matter resolved before we might meet again."

Benny nodded. "Okay. Fine! I like a partner who isn't afraid of dirtying his hands himself. We'll keep in touch then." Benny shook Leland's hand.

"Yes, we will," Leland assured him.

Chipper Tampered with Evidence

Next on the docket, Leland needed to check on Ralph Bunch.

Walking up through the firs, Leland heard what sounded like clicking sounds with rasping breaths but saw nothing. He approached the tall cottage of cedar shakes and irregular rock and mortar walls with tall, north facing windows, knocked on the doorsill and called out. Stepping through the north facing cottage's open door, he found Ralph munching on a bowl of bamboo sprouts and obviously trying to mimic the loud sounds coming from the stereo. Chopped pieces of boiled egg, and various sprouts and nuts filled other bowls of nibbles set there on the table. The chipping sounds went ballistic. Ralph turned. Leland covered his ears while Ralph turned the stereo's volume down.

"I miked Chipper, there." Ralph pointed. "A lot of their communication is carried in nuances of tone." Ralph pointed upwards to a chipmunk who had scurried up the walls upon Leland's entry and was hiding in the rafters. "He's not used to visitors. Just a second."

Ralph placed thumbs and forefingers to both sides of his head with fingers outstretched and then closed his eyelids slightly as if in thought and glanced upwards. The chipmunk froze and 'listened'.

"This," Ralph glanced to Leland and wiggled his fingers, "is just for show. It's my way of saying, 'Concentrate. I'm sending a message your way.' And then Chipper stops whatever he is doing to pick up my mental broadcast. It works fairly well. He'll be fine now." Ralph nodded to the chipmunk above his head. "If you're a safe thing, I picture a cashew. If you're a threat, I image a hawk." Ralph gave Leland a big ol' manly pat on the back. "You're just a big ol' cashew."

"Thanks," Leland responded uncomfortably. It was unusual for Ralph to be 'physical'.

From what the postman, Bill Parsons, had said, Leland was expecting a half-crazed Ralph. But from the look of both Ralph and the small cottage, he was doing fine. In fact, the cottage looked more together than it had seemed in years. The panes of window which looked out on the valley were all spotlessly clean. The place was swept and dusted. The dishes were washed and set to dry neatly in the rack. Paintings were stacked neatly against the walls or hung in blank areas. In fact, Ralph was different. He stood different. He spoke different.   And, it looked like Ralph's whole oeuvre had changed. Energy suffused the paintings. The colors were brighter. Leland looked closer. The brushwork was vigorous and the coloring more dramatic.   Leland didn't see any whiskey bottles or beer cans littering the area and Ralph himself was smiling.

"It's true. I seem to have found a new vigor for life," Ralph himself commented freely, straightening his shoulders.   "I'm just chewing it up! Couldn't be more happy if I tried to imagine it myself," he admitted, clapping, then headed for the liquor cabinet. "Let's celebrate!"

One truly odd thing was the cases of canned nuts and jars of boiled eggs stacked up and down the counter. "Chipper says it's going to be a hard winter," Ralph explained. "How about a whiskey?" He glanced out the window, while reaching up to open the cupboard door. "I'd say the sun is well across the yardarm."

Leland spoke up. "From what Parsons had to say, I thought I'd better drive up. You seemed to have scared him pretty good. I'd half expected a raving lunatic."

Ralph poured two fingers into two clean tumblers and handed one to Leland.

"That pussy!" Ralph chortled. "Honest, Leland. All I had to do was smile." Ralph shook his head and took a good swallow.

"Well. That's what he said too," Leland agreed, resting one hand on his belt while he sipped.

Leland couldn't get over the change in Ralph.

"And the crazy hoot fell right over onto his back! I guess when I stepped forward to help him up, he thought I was going for him and scurried off." Ralph whisked the memory away with his fingertips. "He dropped my package, which he wasn't going to deliver. So I just picked it up and walked back here to the studio."

"You know, you are different." Leland eyed Ralph.

Ralph nodded and for a moment mused on his brand new bright red checkered shirt. "You don't have to tell me. But then, I think 'Chipper', up there, has had a lot to do with it. Really getting close to nature can change a man, Leland. And vice versa, I'd suppose."

Leland showed his puzzlement.

"Chipper, up there, has changed a lot too!"

"Ummm," said Leland glancing up at Chipper's two small beady black eyes taking in the room. "How so?"

Ralph covered his brushes and palette with saran wrap and indicated that they should move into the den area just a step away where two soft leather chairs were arranged by a wood stove, which had a summertime tin of fresh wildflowers set on the top. As Leland sat and settled in, Ralph positioned himself with one elbow on the arm of the chair, as if to note that what he had to say next was confidential.

"Chipper was an orphan when we found each other. Had been nearly since birth. Hawk got both his folks. One, one day, and the other not a week later." Ralph sighed. "And he'd been living in a state of terror ever since! Couldn't trust a shadow to save himself. Took to only revealing himself at night. I know because I receive his dreams." Ralph's eyes grew. "Not a pretty life for a kid. And then," Ralph leaned in further, "it looked to me like he came upon a murder. It's pretty dark and there are the shadows of these two men. And flashes! Like a gun muzzle. It seemed to me that it might have to do with one of these murders you'd been investigating."

Leland glanced up. "He's a witness?"

Ralph nodded. "He thinks so. I mean, I'd guess as much. You want some more?"

Leland held out his glass, and Ralph poured them both another two knuckles worth.

"I didn't know quite what to do about it. So I figured that until you'd caught the guys, I'd kinda keep him in witness protection." Ramey looked slightly embarrassed to be admitting his failure to assist.

Leland nodded.

"It was a very odd situation, you have to admit," Ralph wheedled.

Leland nodded.

"And then, there was this thing that I was afraid might get him," Ralph nodded to Chipper, "into some trouble."

"And that was?" Leland studied Ralph, who was studying Chipper, then leaned in closer to hear.

"Well." Ralph hesitated before leaning away a bit as if to say it more safely, "He tampered with evidence."

"Tampered with the *body*?"

Ralph nodded slightly. "I believe he ate some. Maybe the brains? It was very dark and hard to tell. But I could tell you what it tasted like."

Leland set his drink, then pushed it away.

Back at the Campaign Café

After leaving Ralph's the first thing Leland did was to phone Merlin. He pushed a branch away as he strode down the overgrown path. "Could you meet me for a cup of coffee at the Café?"

"When?" Merlin asked. Leland heard a calf bawling in the background.

"Whenever you're free. I should be there all afternoon."

"Okay. I'll see what I can do." Merlin rang off.

While driving into town, Leland was hoping his phone call would accomplish two things. First, he needed Merlin to check out the bodies over at Smither's to make sure the freezer was locked and sealed with no way for the contents to leak out or any varmint to creep in. And second, he wanted to notify whoever it was who ran Perez, that he wanted to set up a meeting at the Café'. Leland figured the fellow would be reasonably jumpy about meeting with him alone in his detached 'temporary' quarters. He (or she) would probably be thinking that the Sheriff's behavior was unpredictable and that he might end up being shot, just as Perez had. So Leland reasoned that whoever it was might try to make contact - if they met in some place busy and safe. The Café' was the only busy spot in town. And the smell of biscuits and coffee would make any man feel safe, wouldn't it?

At least until that person looked out upon the blackened wreckage of what used to be the sheriff's offices just across the street. Leland looked out as he passed into town. Yellow tape ringed it. Two kids with bicycles were staring across the tape at the burned mess. One poked at something with a stick. Then a tourist bus pulled out from just up the street and lumbered past blocking the view as Leland pulled into a slot before the Café'.

There were people inside of the Café' and Leland recognized all of them as locals. Some nodded as he passed. Leland nodded at Carmella's worried countenance, indicating he'd be at the end table by the far window. Then he grabbed a discarded newspaper off the counter and sat down to wait. It wasn't long before Carmella approached.

"Coffee Leland?"

"Please."

Carmella leaned in as she poured. "Listen Leland. I feel terrible. I had no *idea* that man was a serial killer."

Leland looked up. "I never figured you did, Carmella."

"You must think I have terrible taste in men," she said, automatically smoothing her blouse and repairing her bust line as she half sat.

Leland thought about that. He considered Peter Barnett, her husband/mayor, and Stan, serial killer, and then a long list of others, and found his mind wandering back...

"You don't have to say it." There was nothing more to pour, so Carmella sat opposite, with her back to the room.

"There's no rhyme nor reason to who we're attracted to, Carmella." Leland smiled slightly.

"Boy is that the truth! You've said a mouthful there, Leland," Carmella agreed, brushing back a strand of hair. "So. We're okay, then. We're good?" Her big, liquid eyes examined him intently.

"We're fine." Leland patted her hand.

She nodded. "So it's not like you're sore at me for blowing up your offices then?" Carmella grimaced slightly, tilting her head to indicate the wreckage across the way.

Leland gazed at it through the window. Seen through the glass of the window it was like a former life; someplace you could see and remember but not get to. Things would be different now. They already were.

"No," he said. "Not at all. Sooner or later," he added, "everything has to go."

"Yeah. With a bang!" Carmella's hands shot up. She tried a slight chuckle.

Leland nodded.

Carmella sat and watched him for a while, until Leland couldn't sip anymore coffee and she was making him nervous. His brows rose.

"So, we're good then?"

"Yeah."

"Okay. Fine then." Carmella's hands smoothed the gingham table cloth. She leaned in slowly as she began to speak. "Because there's something else, Leland."

Meetings Over Coffee

"I think I might be pregnant," Carmella confided.

Leland spluttered.

"What? Is that funny?"

"No. No," Leland wiped his eyes and blew his nose and held up a hand. "It's just that my thoughts were as far from that as is probably humanly possible," he averred.

"Believe me. So were mine!" Carmella insisted. "Maybe I figured I was too old, or I have just been married too long and gotten too *casual*." Camella's fingers flew about all scattered as if she were trying to think. Then they straightened her hair.

"And you think Stan might be the father?" Leland concluded.

"Well, I probably wouldn't be bringing it up, if it were Peter, now would I?" Carmella snapped, then retreated quickly. "Sorry. Sorry! I didn't mean to be so nasty. It's just that it's a lot to have on my mind, especially at a time like this."

"...at a time like this?" Leland queried further.

"Because there's more!" Carmella grabbed both of Leland's hands in a desperate gesture as she leaned forward to whisper.

Leland was reconsidering his notion of meeting Perez' handler here. Or of doing anything here. Too much was going on. Perhaps going back to the cottage would be better.

"I think Peter has gotten connected in with the Mob. I think Peter is involved with the Mob!"

Leland listened. Carmella went on to describe her recent phone calls to Peter in Fernley, Nevada - a little town just outside of Reno. She reconstructed the events. She told him about Benny's appearance at the restaurant. She even divulged the 'possibility' of Peter's expropriation of funds and "malfeasance", as she called it. "Though, I have to say, I still feel like a bit of a traitor divulging all of this to you. You being, as you are, the Sheriff." She batted her eyes. Leland knew she couldn't help the flirting, and probably didn't even know that she had done it. She smiled.

Leland assessed what he had heard. So Peter had a gambling problem, and now the city had a 'liquidity' problem, he thought. He stirred his coffee, as Carmella moved away to serve others.

"So what do you think?" Carmella breathed the words in a rush, soon as she returned. She looked as though she were hoping Leland had fixed it by then.

"I think it's probably a good thing they did blow up my offices, as the town probably couldn't have paid the rent and utilities anyway. In fact, it's crossing my mind right now that I might be a Sheriff without a paycheck."

"That's all you can think of?!" Carmella rose. "Here I am, running this place all on my own, with a baby in the oven, a serial killer for a father, a husband who's an embezzler with a gambling problem, all steaming in a thick stew of 'mob-involvement', and that's all you've got to say?!" Carmella heard her voice rise in spite of herself. "And you're worried about your little, teensy, almost insignificant, Sheriff's paycheck?" She hissed, making a little space between her thumb and forefinger, as women will do when dismissing a man' penis size.

Leland drew back.

Carmella immediately realized what she had done and readjusted herself. "I'm sorry. I'm sorry! My bad again! And again!! I don't know what's wrong with me." She began to sob. "I'm falling apart!"

Leland tried to console her, but she ran off into the kitchen, all the while trying to adjust her bust line.

She didn't come back for a while. And in the meantime, not having anything else to do, Leland assumed the waitress duties, getting people their checks, serving the food and coffee and explaining away the event in lightly timed references to women's 'issues' and such. "They go a little crazy," he said. Others nodded, some even adding their own tales beginning with "nothing surprises me anymore..." Most took it "for what it was worth", as they had been in here many times before and had witnessed other of

Carmella's meltdowns.

When finally Carmella did return, most of the customers who had witnessed the event had left, and the new crew knew nothing of it. So Carmella resumed her duties with a freshly made up face. And Leland resumed his coffee and the (other) news.

It wasn't long before Merlin appeared.

Merlin Appears

Merlin looked wiped out. His trousers were a mess and some manure and straw still clung to a boot. A trickle of blood had run down his forehead, most likely from smacking his head on some barn stall. His hands were freshly washed however.

"You look exhausted," Leland noted.

"Thanks! I've been up all night, and then some." Merlin blinked, raising his eyelids as far as humanly possible while glancing down. "But, got 'er done!" He grinned at Leland.

Leland smiled.

"Cutest little heifer you'll ever see, after we cleaned her all up and put her next to mom in some fresh hay."

"You want some coffee?"

"Nah. I'm just about to call it a day. On my way to tuck myself in right after this."

"You got the energy left for one more important errand?"

Merlin smiled and inhaled. "I'm guessing you wouldn't ask unless it was something of real importance so, yes."

"Good.   I much appreciate it." Leland leaned in closer to confer. "Now here is what's going on."

Leland explained to Merlin all about Ralph Bunch and his pet chipmunk, Chipper.

"And so Ralph has him in 'Witness Protection'?" Merlin laughed.

"It's funny, but it's not." Leland looked grim. "If any sort of varmints around here manage to get into those corpses somehow over at Smither's - or, if there's a leak in the containment for any reason… well, we could have a real *something* on our hands."

"Yeah. Okay. I got it." Merlin nodded. "You just want me to drop by and double check that everything's secure."

"…contained and locked," Leland added.

"Contained and locked," Merlin repeated. He rose.

"Thanks," Leland said.

"You're welcome as always Leland," Merlin called as he left the Café'.

Mister Big

After Merlin left, Leland glanced around. A few afternoon stragglers remained over their coffees as did Leland. Only one cook labored behind the carousel, and he didn't look like he was working very hard. Leland noticed the cook adjust his glasses, as he pulled an order.

"A piece of pie? You want a piece of pie?" He shouted in Spanish.

Carmella shouted something back, from the restroom.

"I'm the line cook back here, in the *back*, you know? I cook things! This pie slice you want? It's baked goods. Plus, it's *already* cooked."

"Give me that!" Carmella tore the slip from the cooks hand and went about collecting a slice of pie from off the covered counter pedestal, slipping it onto a plate. "I've got too much on my mind for this," she grumbled, wrist snap sliding the pie down the counter without looking. The customer blocked it just before it collided with his coffee.

"Thanks?" He remarked.

Carmella walked through to the back and disappeared.

"Sweet Virgin preserve us," the cook whispered, in whining English this time, crossing himself several times.

Leland continued reading his newspaper. He glanced out the window next and saw that a new car had pulled up - a black Prius. But the older, skinny man inside appeared to have fallen asleep, or was taking a cat nap with a cap pulled down over his eyes. Leland observed a while then turned back to his paper. A fellow was standing next to his booth. "You mind if I join you?" He asked.

"I'm waiting to meet someone…"

"I figured as much." The man nodded, seating himself and slapping down his folded newspaper. "You don't use your cell for a couple weeks. Then you call up a friend to tell him you'll be spending the afternoon at the Campaign Café in downtown Kimmel. It sounded an awful lot like an invitation." He cast Leland a thin smile.

"It was." Leland nodded, assessing the fellow. Leland had learned never to judge a fellow by their looks; to wait until you've seen them move. But he had to think the fellow was no real physical threat. He was tall but he couldn't have weighed over 120 and was probably at least 60. He looked like an English professor who lived on coffee, crackers and vegetable spreads. He wore corduroys and a patterned dress shirt, a belt that stretched pelvic prominence to pelvic prominence, and Dockers with wool socks. He had thining, salt and pepper, formerly reddish curls, thin lips, neck folds and facial creases from smiling a lot *with chilling bemusement*, Leland would have guessed. "What can I do for you?"

"The eggs here. Are they free-ranged?" His guest studied the menu, not looking at Leland.

"Yeah. But I'd go with the caged."

The man pursed his lips. "Why's that?"

"The Bentleys let them eat what they can peck out of the county dump. Whereas the Hartley's keep theirs caged and feed them the regular stuff."

The man regarded the menu with disdain.

Leland considered the man. "Though I've never looked much into what the chicken feed is made from," he continued. "Who are you?"

"I'm a person you want to talk to," the man replied, setting the menu.

"Good." Leland motioned to Carmella.

Carmella appeared. "What do you want?"

Leland nodded to the man, who he had decided - because he wouldn't have believed whatever name the fellow gave him anyway - to call, "Ogilvie".

Ogilvie said, "Oatmeal with skim milk, please."

Carmella waited, tapping her foot.

"Some oatmeal with skimmed milk," Leland repeated the order, wondering where in the world Carmella's attention was.

Carmella paused before writing. "You're kidding me. Oatmeal with skimmed milk? That's what you've waited all afternoon in a restaurant for?"

"I've heard the waitresses in these fly-over areas of the country can be a little testy, but she seems especially abrasive," Ogilvie noted.

"She's had a hard morning."

"Is that it?" Carmella was rocking on her back foot. "Cause' I'm in no mood to sit here listening to you mumble and lisp."

'More coffee', Leland indicated by lifting his cup.

Carmella poured and left, her hips swinging purposefully.

"She's punched the tickets of most every rustic in this town, I'd guess." Ogilvie whistled lowly. Then he glanced at the back of his hands which he had arranged face down on the table top, then looked up meaningfully at Leland. "You have killed several of my men," Ogilvie spoke slowly and sternly.

"Just one," Leland corrected him.

"Just one?"

"Because he was getting hysterical."

"*Hysterical?* That's an odd choice of words. Because I don't believe I've ever heard of anybody dispatching one of my men for being '*hysterical*'." He glanced around. "You kill people around here for that?"

"Seven dead people, an exploded Sheriff's office, and a crashed van load of Japanese tourists. All in the service of keeping your operations quiet. I'd call that an hysterical over-reaction by any reach of the imagination," Leland countered. "Agent Perez was way off the reservation."

"And so you felt you had to kill him." Ogilvie's blue eyes pierced Leland's composure. "But you don't even know which "*reservation*" he was on - or off - do you? Or *what* the intended extent of his activities was meant to be?"

Leland paused for a sip of coffee and stared out the window at the remains of his offices. Another tour bus was stopped and giving the context.

"So how do *you* fire people in *your* line of work?" Leland asked.

Ogilvie's brows rose in surprise. He gazed out where Leland was looking.

"Point taken," he said.

"So what about my other two men?" Ogilvie asked, after Carmella had come and gone with the skimmed milk and oatmeal.

"Near as I can tell, Harriet Weeds most likely shot them and fed them to their hogs," Leland stated.

Mr. Ogilvie's frown deepened and his eyes took on a steely glint. "And she and her husband are the ones shot by your colleague, Agent Hailey?"

Leland nodded.

"Who are currently residing in a frozen meat locker of a Mr. Vernon Smithers," Mr. Ogilvie said.

Leland nodded. "Along with two of the serial killer's victims."

"Which makes six. And where is Agent Perez, currently?"

"His remains are still being processed." Leland nodded.

Ogilvie pushed the oatmeal away, setting his spoon. He rolled his eyes, while leaning back and reaching into his jacket pocket for a cigarette. He halted. "You aren't going to shoot me and feed *me* to the hogs are you?"

"Not unless I have to. Or feel like it," Leland added.

"Well, thank God! You don't have to," Ogilvie said, while fishing out his cigarettes and lighting up. "Filthy habit," he waved the cigarette, "which I only indulge when I'm having conversations like this - in the *homeland*." He assessed Leland. "So. What do you want *Mister* Sheriff Leland Kelly? I'm assuming you called me here for some reason. Are you applying for Agent Perez's job?" He smiled offhand.

The thought hadn't occurred to Leland. But when it did, it was a good one.

"Yes." Leland nodded, adopting the idea. "I am applying for Agent Perez' job."

Ogilvie coughed. He laughed. He put out his smoke. "I thought I was joking," he said.

Leland shrugged.

Ogilvie assessed him all over again. "You don't even know who I represent - that is, *if* I represent anyone other than myself."

Leland raised his palms.

Ogilvie smiled and nodded. "And you don't have any idea what you'd be required to do?"

"I figured I could tell you that." Leland grinned.

Ogilvie bounced against the booth backing and laughed. "By God man." He shook his head.

Leland figured this might be his best moment for his pitch. "Look. So far what have you gotten for your effort? You've gotten seven deaths, a letter of inquiry from the Japanese Ambassador, a blown apart sheriff's offices - right in the heart of downtown Kimmel, from which tours encapsulating the whole sorry episode depart five days a week on an hourly basis - *plus* involvement of the New York Times." Leland counted off. "What *I've* got is a knowledge of this county and these people, and more importantly - *control of the investigation.* Which is something you've wanted to create all along by killing people. Am I right?" Leland's ire began to show.

Leland's tone of voice drew some attention from the other Café patrons.

"You know, this idea about covert ops that violence is our option of first resort is truly *not* the case. It's expensive. It's high risk. It's high *exposure.*" Ogilvie made a cathedral of his palms.

Leland swore.

Ogilvie indicated that Leland should calm down. "We just don't need it."

Leland nodded emphatically. "You're preaching to the choir

here," he hissed. "Just give me the job, and you'll get what you want."

"How do you know what 'we' want?"

"I figure you want what I want."

"And what do you want?"

"I want you all to go away!"

Ogilvie shook his head with what might have amounted to a grin.

"Plus, a few more things."

"And those would be?" Ogilvie tapped his lips with a forefinger.

Negotiations

"First off, I don't want any more killings and violence in my county."

Ogilvie smiled. "We couldn't be more in agreement. In fact, stopping these killings is what brought upon our involvement in the first place. We have been trying to call it all off since Stan first surfaced out here."

"You've created the deaths of 7 people!"

"And you've *found* the guy who did that," Ogilvie responded. "It seems to me we're working towards the same ends here."

"That's just what Agent Perez said."

"*Before* you shot him."

"Yeah." Leland nodded.

Ogilvie stared at Leland

Ogilvie toyed with the oatmeal, took a few bites, then pushed it away. "Look," he said. "We don't *want* any more of these people killed - and I'll tell you *why*."

Leland sighed, people were handing him garbage, but unwrapping it from the finest cloth. "You know, talking with you is just like talking to a criminal. They don't share anything. So then I put the screws to them, and they give me a little, then claim, "That's it." So I screw down a little harder, and they give me a little more and say, "But I swear, that's all!" Leland shook his head. "It's all garbage. And I just *hate* picking through it."

"It's *because*, we were successful." Ogilvie shook his head. "Our people have successful detached the mind from its substrate! Which means…" Ogilvie's eyes wandered upwards for a moment as if envisioning a grand new future. "First. That the *last* thing we want to do is to kill any more of these people, who are 'specially' gifted."

"That's the same thing Stan said," Leland remembered. "Because it was looking to him like he couldn't figure out where their minds were going to pop up next. "

"That's right," Ogilvie said.

"The mind of the woman Stan killed, cold-cocked him with a shovel. I'd wager that the 'wandering mind' of *that* woman would be *real* happy to find you," Leland added. He took a sip of his coffee and watched Ogilvie's brows crease.

"So you do know where Stan is?" Ogilvie said.

Leland was mute.

Ogilvie shook his head then leaned in to speak: "Right now, we've got their testimony trapped within their original body. We kill them, and their knowledge is as likely to drift anywhere and re-attach to whatever substrate it can. So we won't know where this information is or where it could end up. And this is critical."

Ogilvie waited, until Leland nodded.

"As soon as we have a success in this business, we start creating a back story - that is, a legal way to have created whatever it is our tech boys have cooked up. Then, once the science of our 'discovery' is 'vetted', we can bring it to market and really *change the world*!" Ogilvie grinned. The light in his eyes was messianic.

But Ogilvie waited, until Leland reacted.

Leland nodded.

"For Godsakes man, get excited!" Ogilvie scolded. "Do you think that we are planning to attach the mind of a human to a squirrel? You drove here. What did you see on the way?"

"Normal stuff," Leland answered, "Forest. Pastures. Cows. Trees…"

"That's right," Ogilvie continued scolding. "Trees. Grass. *Plants!* Do you realize that there are aspens whose groves communicate by virtue of their roots over square miles? Do you realize that there are fungi who do this and whose mass extends hundreds of square miles? Did you know that a bean plant, when viewed in time lapse photography does not happen upon its pole by random search - but grows directly towards it? What you are seeing out there," Ogilvie tossed his hand towards the window, "is an *enormous* computer - all powered by sunlight! Just because *it*," he indicated the outdoors outside the window, "has no consciousness, doesn't mean it's not damn smart. *We* plan to supply the consciousness."

He continued. "But first, the by-products of the original research need to be collected and swept up so that there are not any loose ends. And that is what Stan has been out there creating for us, is loose ends… *very* loose ends. He thought he was eliminating them for us. Our bad. It was a miscommunication. Nevertheless, we need to 'neutralize' this Stan, before more damage is done. He has become a loose end himself. And, we also are going to need a place to store all of these former test subjects of ours. Which brings me to an offer."

Leland's brows rose.

"Kimmel County *could* become the prime district - or *prime repository* - to place former test subjects. It's a rural, remote, but pleasant locale. We could offer them a quiet life as long as they remain within Kimmel County boundaries. Nobody needs killing. And you watch over their welfare. Any problems, and all of our resources are at your disposal."

"So, I'd be more like a *warden* than a Sheriff?" Leland took another sip of his coffee.

"In some manner. Only one which is *preventing* a lot of killing, and is very well paid, and a real rainmaker for Kimmel County." Ogilvie gazed up and down the street outside the Café windows. "I'd guess Kimmel could use some money?"

Leland thought about it. "Everyone wants a piece of this place all of a sudden," he observed.

"How so?"

"A syndicate from down south wants to bring gambling into Kimmel."

"I can't see a need for that," Ogilvie said coolly.

Leland considered this. He saw Carmella bussing some dishes. He saw a few hard working farmers. Then his attention was distracted by the noise and sounds of a busload of camera toting tourists lumbering past outside. He turned his gaze back towards Ogilvie.

"Neither can I." Leland agreed.

"What did you say to this Syndicate?" Ogilvie pressed him.

"I said, I'd think about it."

"And what did they say?"

"The man smiled and said that I could think about it as long as I want, as long as the answer was "yes"."

"And how did you like that?"

"Not very much."

"And when was this?"

"He dropped by just the other day."

Ogilvie played with the oatmeal bowl, sliding it back and forth with his palms as he thought. "I'll tell you what," he said. "I'll get rid of this mob guy for you for three reasons. The first is to demonstrate to you the power of the organization which backs me. I need to convince you that there is no other credible way of solving your problems than except working with me, rather than against me. You can't just keep killing us; it's futile. The second is, if we're going to do business, I don't want this backwater polluted by organized crime and gambling. We want it rural and *quiet*. And third, think of it as your first down payment."

Leland nodded. "There's one more thing."

Ogilvie nodded. "We need to have Stan."

Odds and Ends

Merlin did as Leland asked. He dropped by Vern Smithers' to check on the security of the corpses. They were all just laid on top of one another in black, rubbery body bags and stuck together like steaks with freezer burn. Digging with bare fingers through a thick hoarfrost, Merlin broke Nancy's body bag loose and unzipped it. After some serious tugging on the zipper and rolling up his sleeves to get his hands in, he felt around. Orienting his hands as his cold fingers drifted over her face, nostrils, lips, around a cheek, past an ear with it's cold tiny nob of a little pearl earring and then to the sharp edge of a broken skull, he came to the irregular shape of squeezed and scooped brains frozen hard as chunks of concrete. After blowing on his cold hands till feeling returned, Merlin grabbed a small axe he had lifted from Vern's tool wall and by making quick, constricted whacks without being able to see what he was whacking inside of the tight confines of the bag, he was able to chip off what he believed to be a sizeable chunk. He slipped this chunk of Nancy Loomis into a zip lock sack he had in his pocket for specimens, then blew on his hands again. Then he put everything back as it was and, after checking around the rear, sides and bottom of the locker for leaks or any signs of vermin, secured the latch. He walked out as he had entered, nodding to Vern, standing at the counter, as he left.

The specimen thawed in his pocket on the drive home. Merlin toyed with it as he thought and as he drove. It grew soft, then squishy. This was a big decision. Not one to be taken lightly. What Merlin intended could have immense consequences - at least for himself. But there was really no decision to be made. Merlin knew what he was bound to do. There was no way he wouldn't. When he got home, he walked immediately to the bathroom, stripped and took a long, hot shower. Then he mixed the thawed packet of brains with some warming milk on the stove. Then, when it was lukewarm, he drank the whole mixture. Then, having to chew slightly as it went down, he swallowed afterwards and belched slightly.

The next day, a New Jersey resident, Mr. Cenza, took a look at his bank account online and found 32 dollars and 13 cents. This concerned him. Normally he had around 60 million. He made some calls. The persons he called were still working the problem. When Mr. Cenza consulted his bank account the second day he found only the 13 cents and a note that said, "Leave Kimmel County."

A day or so later in Las Vegas, Lazlo took a call from New Jersey. "Mister Cenza. Always good to hear from you. How are you?"

"Who gives a fuck how I am," his boss answered. "What I need to know, and right now, is what you got going out in someplace called *Kimmel*. That's a town, right?"

"Yeah. Yeah! That's a town," Lazlo blurted.

"What in the hell are you doing there?"

"Doing there," Lazlo repeated.

"Yeah. *Doing there*. Don't play a dumbass. What the hell? You're bringing down the mountain on me. Outta some place like Kimmel? That's also a county, right?"

"Yeah. Yeah! It's also a county."

"What the fuck?!"

"I don't know," Lazlo considered. "But no problems, as far as I knew. Benny Green. You know Benny Green from up that way?"

"Yeah, I know the Greenman."

"Well. He and I, we're working on a deal to expand our gambling enterprise there. A pretty good deal it looks like. Only one sheriff. No business to speak of but near enough to a big population center. We figure we can own the place for almost nothing. The mayor owes us quite a chunk. Last word I had from Benny was that things were going well, and that he'd spoken with the Sheriff about breaking ground, a new Sheriff's facility and all that…"

"Well. I don't want that, okay?"

"Can I ask why? Because we've already made a fairly sizable investment."

"Have you made a 60 million dollar investment?"

"No, nothing like that."

"Well, it appears I have. So I don't care! You hear that. I don't want you there. I don't want Benny there. I don't want anybody associated with you there, or anybody who knows me, or anybody who's even thought about me being there or thinking about doing any business there. Draw like a big red circle around it on your map if you have to, like it's the world's biggest hemorrhoid! But nobody goes there anymore okay? It's absolutely off-limits. Got that!"

"Yeah, sure." Lazlo nodded vigorously. "But I'm telling ya, all there is there is just this one horse town with a single Sheriff. Benny described it all to me over the phone."

"Well it's the pimple on a much bigger ass. So you just pull out and stay away! You got that? NOBODY crosses that county line!"

"Yeah, I got that."

"And tell Benny."

"Sure. Will do." Lazlo paused. "He'll want to drive back and get his money out."

"How much money?"

"Five million in cash. We figured it's a sure way to launder a lot of money, risk free."

"Apparently it's *not* risk free, now is it?"

"I guess not," Lazlo agreed. "But what do I tell Benny? He's not going to like leaving five million."

"Well tell Benny, that if he owns this mayor so much, to have the mayor bring the money back to him!"

"Alright. I can do that."

"See that you do. And quickly," Cenza added.

Cenza went back to his computer. He pressed "Reply" and typed in: "We're out!" Then he hit send.

By the next day, he had his 32 dollars back and a nice "Thank You." It was less than gratifying. The day after that though, he had his 60 million back. Plus a smiley face! This was much more gratifying.

Not much later Peter Barnett got a phone call from Benny Green. "Hi, remember me?"

Peter nodded.

"Hey? ...you there?"

"Uh, yes. Yes, I remember you." Peter sighed.

"Good. That's real good, 'cause I need to give you some instructions."

"Let me just get a pen and a piece of paper," Peter sighed again. He had just gotten up with a bad hangover and had been staring morosely into a cup of warmed up old coffee when the phone had rung. Apparently Carmella had gotten herself pregnant by the serial killer. She wasn't thrilled with the business arrangements Peter had struggled to achieve. She was going to stop running things at the Café. She'd said it was his turn to take over management, as she was "with child". And she was cutting her hours. Plus, she'd told the Sheriff about the town's money shortfall. So, Peter felt with all of this on his mind, plus the hangover, a pen and a piece of paper were warranted. He walked away from the phone, acquired what he needed, sat down slowly and said, "Shoot."

"You sound like you wished I would," Benny offered.

"Let's say I've had better mornings," Peter said.

"Misery loves company apparently, 'cause things aren't turning up too rosy here either. My partner in Vegas says that the proposed venture is off, that word is down from headquarters. We are to shut down our operations in Kimmel. You know of any reason for that?"

Peter was writing, "You know any reason for that?" when he realized what Benny was asking.

"The development is off?" Peter responded.

"Yes! The 'development', our relationship, everything... It's now off the table. I asked, "Would you know any reason for that?" Just, by the way, you know..." Benny tapped his fingers. 'What a run around', he thought. 'And all this catch up isn't making me any money.'

"No. No reason I know of," Peter said mystified.

"Okay. I didn't figure you would. But anyway, here's what I want you to do. You got that pencil and piece of paper?"

"Yeah."

"Good. So here it is. I want you to go get that 5 million I gave you, put it in the trunk of your car and drive it to Warren, which is just one mile east of the Kimmel county line. I'll meet you there at the Daybreak Café, where we can meet to drive someplace and exchange it."

"For what?"

"For what? For your life, I'd suppose. What I mean is, where we'll take the money from the trunk of your automobile and place it into the trunk of mine - leaving the trunk of yours completely empty." Benny paused. "You got that all written down?"

"Uh yeah, sure," Peter said.

"Good. See you there in an hour."

"That's pretty quick," Pete said.

"So drive fast!" Benny answered.

Peter and the Money

Peter rushed about, getting dressed and loading the money into the trunk of the old Oldsmobile. Which wasn't hard. He hadn't taken the money out of the trunk yet, not having thought of a good place for hiding it. Instead, he just parked the car behind the garage and had covered it with a mossy green tarp. Now it was a simple matter to just uncover the car and - begging the question as to whether it would start or not - drive it to Warren.

The car started. Peter backed it out, slammed the transmission into drive, and with a quick 'chirp' of the tires and a short 'cough' of the engine headed down their oiled street towards the highway for Warren. By the time he was halfway there though, Peter had collected his thoughts enough to consider that he might be acting rashly. After all, he did have the 5 million. He pulled the old car off the road to think. 'Isn't possession nine-tenths of the law?' He considered.

'But, of course, that was the point. There *was* no law in this matter,' the more prudent side of his nature argued. 'There was only being killed or not being killed.'

Peter had never been one much to give into the more prudent side of his nature. In truth, it was the smaller side, whenever the other side was staring at hard cash.

'You've got to admit,' he thought, arguing with himself. 'Five million would solve nearly every problem I have. Especially, since Benny has decided not to conduct further business in Kimmel.'

On the other hand, 'Getting killed would end *absolutely* every problem you have,' his smaller, but more insistent side shrieked.

Peter sat there conflicted, undecided, until, looking down at this watch he realized that his hour had passed. 'Best to call Benny than to have him call me,' he thought.

Peter called Benny. "Hey!" he said.

"Hey yourself," Benny growled.

"Problem. Sorry I'm late."

"Where are you?"

Peter looked around. "I'm about 3 miles west of where we are to meet," he said. "The, *tire* went flat."

"The… *tire* went flat," Benny repeated. "So. Have you fixed it? Are you *on your way*?"

"Well, no. Not yet."

"So. You're thinking it's *going to fix itself*?" Benny shook his head.

"No. No. It won't do that," Pete acknowledged meekly.

"So get out and fix it and drive here like we planned! And do it quickly." Benny hung up.

Peter rang him back. "Okay," he said.

Peter hung up. Then he sat for thirty seconds and then rang Benny back again.

"Okay, again. Well, here's the thing. I was thinking, since I'm not very good with this sort of thing anyway, and it may take me some time, and since you seem to be in a hurry, maybe you'd like to drive *here*, where we could do the exchange?"

"But I don't want to drive there," Benny declared.

"But it's only 3 miles," Peter said.

"I don't care," Benny declared. "You just drive that wreck of a car on the rim if you have to, but get yourself over here and now." Benny hung up.

Peter sat for another while. Then he called back. "Hello again. Another problem," he said.

Benny sighed.

"The spare tire and jack are under all the money."

"Yeah?"

"Well. What am I to do? Unload it all and stack it alongside the highway while I fix my tire? And I don't suppose I could get more than 100 yards on the rim."

Benny looked at his phone. He wished he could have reached through it to bitch slap that pissy little excuse for a human being on the other end of the line, but he couldn't. "So what do you propose?"

"Drive here," Peter suggested for the second time. "You can be here in a few minutes! I can roll off the roadway enough on the rim to find us a spot to exchange the money. Then you can be on your way, and I can call a wrecker."

"Let me call you back," Benny said.

Benny speed dialed Lazlo. Lazlo heard him out. Then Lazlo speed dialed Cenza. Cenza heard him out. "How much money is it?" Cenza asked.

"Five million," Lazlo said.

"I stand to lose 60 million. No deal."

"Benny isn't going to like this. I mean, he's standing 3 miles away from five million of his own money, and he isn't allowed to go pick it up?" Lazlo argued Benny's case.

"Tell him "No." Someday that guy will want to take his money somewhere where he can have some fun with it, and *then* he can take it away from him. But not before. Got it?"

"Got it," Lazlo sighed. He made the call to Benny.

Benny couldn't believe it. "You're saying you want me to just drive away from five million of my own money?" He asked.

"I'm saying, you will if you want to stay alive," Lazlo answered. "Sorry," he added.

But it was hard for anyone else to really understand Benny's sorrow.

"Okay. Look. Here is how we'll do this," Benny said to Peter over the phone. "Leave the tire flat and the trunk *shut* and call the wrecker. Have the wrecker tow you and your car here to Warren. I'll meet you there at the shop."

"I don't understand why you can't just drive three miles to meet me where I am right now," Peter whined. "So we don't take the risk of dealing with a 3rd party to a car whose trunk load of money is already crushing the rear shocks. It's just a pointless risk," Peter argued.

"The only way I'm going to drive *there*," Benny emphasized, "is if I am headed there to *kill* you, you got that? To put a nice oblong bullet right through your forehead. You got that? So go call that wrecker. And get that pile of bolts towed here to Warren before I lose my patience!"

"I got that," Peter sulked.

"Good," Benny said. Then he clicked off and drove to the only garage in Warren to wait for Peter and his money.

He waited the full day. He called.

Peter never showed. He never answered.

Leland and Stan and Nancy Gillis

Leland drove off to Ramey's after his meeting with Ogilvie. He told them he figured the coast was "as clear as it's ever likely to be". They all had a lot of questions to which Leland said he thought it best for all of their futures that he not answer. And that it was incumbent upon them all to stay mum about all that had happened and to not talk to the press for fear of damaging any agreement he believed had been reached.

Nobody much liked this. Especially Nancy Gillis, their 'embedded' reporter.

"We can talk about it on your way home," Leland said.

"Big truce. They offer probably not to kill us."

"We can talk about it on your way home," Leland repeated. "It's a step ahead of where we *were*," he added.

"You all want to shut me up, to *muffle the Press!*" Nancy stomped.

"You don't have a Press. All you have is your pencil and a spiral bound notebook. Just like I don't have the full force of the law," Leland admonished her. "All I really have is this fairly large gun and my wits. I don't get to do everything I want to do, and you don't get to do everything you want to do. The trick is to get to do as much as is possible. I want to keep this county safe and more or less legal, without getting more people killed doing it. And for your part, you have to decide how much of the truth can get published. People will only stand so much reality. So what part of it do you want to write about?"

"I want to write about my experience of what happened. In fact, I already have." Nancy crossed her arms.

"We'll talk about it on the way home," Leland said.

Nancy Gillis said nothing.

Ruth caught a ride with Agent Hailey back to town. Nancy Loomis began showing Ramey around his home as she discussed how they might handle their new state of affairs. Merlin was home asleep. Leland had Stan in the back as he drove Nancy Gillis home.

"I tell you what," Leland said once he had his schoolgirl reporter in the car. "How would you like to talk to our Mr. Big?"

Nancy looked at Leland doubtfully, thought about it a while, then nodded.

Leland left it at that.

Stan said nothing.

Leland's last task of the day was to hand over Stan. He called his home phone to say he'd be having dinner with a couple friends at the Campaign Café. When he and Stan and Nancy Gillis arrived, Mr. Ogilvie was already in the corner booth. Mr. Ogilvie's brows rose when Leland introduced Nancy Gillis.

"So you're *the* Mr. Big," Nancy said, pulling out her spiral notebook and pencil.

"Not so Big as you might imagine," Mr. Ogilvie responded as they seated themselves.

"Maybe we could talk about that?" Nancy suggested, touching her pencil lead to her tongue.

"That was my plan." Ogilvie smiled.

Leland left them to talk, while he took another table with Stan.

"So. That's the guy who ran me?" Stan nodded.

"Who knows?" Leland shook his head. "But I'm hoping he can hold together our agreement."

Nancy Gillis and Mr. Big

When Carmella appeared, Nancy ordered her usual cheeseburger and fries. Mr. Big said nothing, just regarded her with icy blue eyes. Carmella didn't turn to him or inquire of him. Nancy would have said something, but she figured a grown-up like Mr. Big was fully capable of speaking.

Once Carmella left though, Nancy broke the ice. "For the record, what is your true name?" Nancy asked, pencil poised.

Mr. Ogilvie smiled, glancing at the table where Sheriff Leland sat. "Why don't you call me... Ogilvie?"

"Do you have any identification you can show me?" Nancy asked.

"No I don't."

"Who do you work for?"

"Nobody I can talk about."

"What do you do?"

"Very little I can speak of..."

Nancy rolled her eyes.

"I *contain* things." He spoke with a chill to it.

"Like 'situations'," Nancy suggested, putting the best spin on it in an attempt to warm him up.

"Yes. Like *that*." Ogilvie smiled, a chilling smile.

Nancy drew out her camera. "Would you mind if I took your photo?"

Ogilvie smiled. "Of course."

"Of course, you would mind? Or, 'Of course. Go ahead.'" Nancy asked.

"Please. Be my guest," Ogilvie smiled. "Would you like me to turn my collar up? I also have thick glasses and a hat."

"This will be fine, the way you are," Nancy said, snapping away quickly and efficiently.

The lighting was good. There was enough backlighting from the Café interior for good visualization, and the key light streaming in through the Café windows gave dramatic relief to Ogilvie's skin folds and wrinkles, porous nose and flaring eyebrows. His reddish/grey hair virtually glowed. He was the quintessential covert op and would virtually command the headline above the fold, Nancy imagined as she shot. With a smile, she double checked what she'd shot in the camera's LCD monitor.

Nothing: just the photo of a café booth. In fact, six pictures of a café booth, all nicely lit. Nancy's brows furrowed. She checked the camera. The cap was off. The aperture and speed were appropriate. She looked through the view finder and clicked again. She rechecked the images. Same result.

"It's hard to get a good likeness of me," Ogilvie demurred. "Others have said as much."

Nancy tried again with the same result.

"Are you really *here*?" She grumbled at her malfunctioning camera.

Mr. Ogilvie smiled.

"I guess I'll have to draw you from memory. With words," she said, tucking her camera away.

"I'd guess so," Mr. Ogilvie agreed.

"So. You contain *situations*," Nancy restarted the conversation. "Yes I do."

"And is that what you are doing now?" Nancy asked, pencil poised.

"Yes." Mr. Ogilvie nodded.

Nancy considered. "Well. Before we get to that, can you give me any examples of 'situations' which you have 'contained' in the past? Like references, you know?"

"No, I can't."

"I guess that figures." Nancy nodded.

"Yes," Mr. Ogilvie said.

"You know, a newspaper article usually addresses the questions, Who? What? Where? How? I'd guess we're to How? So. How do you propose to contain *this* situation? Assuming that you are whatever you've said."

"Well," Mr. Ogilvie folded his hands, "I usually present a proposal."

"Let's hear it."

"You are a reporter. You want a story. I'm a spook. I know lots of stories. My proposal is that we work together. You give me something. I give you something."

"But I've already got something."

"Nothing you can publish."

"Watch me."

My Ogilvie did. He gazed at her for some time. Then, just before Nancy was to break the silence, he spoke.

"You have already been published twice in the New York Times," he said.

Nancy nodded.

"Have you ever heard of Henry Hazlitt?"

Nancy shook her head.

"No. I suppose not. You're only 15. And he was well before your time."

`Nancy looked around. Carmella was back hectoring the cook over something, which really wasn't like her. She'd gained a little weight too'.

"Am I boring you?" Mr. Ogilvie had leaned forward.

"Yes, a little," she retorted, returning his look.

"Well good." He pursed his lips. "Because I've found in *my* field, that once I've begun to bore the *News*, then I am on the right track."

Nancy thought about this, then paid greater attention.

"Henry Hazlitt was editorial writer for the New York Times from 1934 till 1945. He argued for a return to the gold standard against the oppositions support for 'fiat' money. That is, money whose price is set by the government."

Nancy yawned.

He shook his head.

"You know, if you really want to be a good reporter you really have to learn to listen through the boring parts," he leaned forward again for emphasis, "because that is when *the Devil is up to his dirty work.*"

Nancy sat up straight as she could to demonstrate attention paid.

"You needn't know anything about monetary policy to understand the point of where I am going with this." He smiled. "The point is, Henry Hazlitt's opinions were judged *old* opinions, whereas those of his opposition were judged *new*. Henry Hazlitt's opinions were not wrong, but they were *out of fashion*. Countries all around us are currently sailing blithely off of financial cliffs for want of following Hazlitt's advice. WWII might have been avoided except for want of following Hazlitt's advice. But that is our point. Henry Hazlitt as editorial writer of the New York Times could not even generate credible opposition to disagree with him. And he was writing for the powerful New York Times. He was just ignored! And it was *because* he was *out of fashion*. So, instead of being congratulated and given a fine raise, our Henry Hazlitt was sacked. The publisher, Arthur Sulzberger, said, upon firing him: "When 43 governments sign an agreement, I don't see how the Times can any longer combat this."

"Okay," Nancy remarked finally.

"I'm telling you this because you appear to be a bright, courageous, *willful* girl - who *is also quite ambitious*. The New York Times will not publish what you are sending them."

Nancy thought about this. "Then why do you care?" She remarked.

Mr. Ogilvie nodded and smiled. "There is a very, narrow window of what is occurring out there, that is, 'the truth', which the New York Times can publish. Otherwise, they will lose their audience. Even if, they would believe *you.*"

"Okay again," Nancy said again. "So why should you care?"

"Because it would be out there!" Mr. Ogilvie's fists pounded the table but, oddly, there was no sound. "*That's* why I'm here. *This* is why I'm taking to you. I am trying to *contain* this situation."

It seemed like Mr. Ogilvie had said most of what he had come to say. So it seemed to Nancy that this might make it a good time for her to think while she finished the remainder of her lunch. She chewed her burger while she observed him. He seemed determined to discipline himself to let time pass. But when she gurgled the straw in her Coke, he was moved to speak - if only to cut through the sound.

"So. You have a choice," Mr. Ogilvie leaned in again. "*You can be this plucky little girl who had a bit of luck getting the inside scoop on some very sensational events and so was rewarded with a byline in the New York Times.* Great! so far. But *then,* who went on to submit a wholly preposterous jumble of 'scoops' about wandering mental states and Secret Government Entities - which no reputable journal would publish and so was left with no job and no audience whatsoever saving a scattered flotilla of crackpots and conspiracy nuts, to whom they are continually dropping by or sending their gibberish." Mr. Ogilvie grinned. "You have no idea how dispiriting that can be - especially to a *good* reporter.   It's like floating round and round in a toilet bowl." He laughed.

Nancy frowned.

Mr. Ogilvie shook his head. He stabbed the table with this index finger. "Reporters are only as good as their sources! You happened upon a sensational series of events, but *you have no sources…* save me. So, in our second scenario this plucky and still ambitious but *wiser* little girl decides that she needs to *cultivate* some of those. *If, she is to happen upon the sorts of stories which can get her back onto the pages of the New York Times.* "

Nancy considered. Much of what he said was probably true. Plus, if she did go ahead and try to publish any of what she had uncovered, it would probably not bode well for any of the others. If she were believed, Sheriff Leland would probably be indicted for murder. Merlin the Veterinarian would be an accomplice. Doctor Ramey and Ralph Bunch and his chipmunk and the Serial Killer Stan would most probably all be killed. She didn't know how Ruth or Agent Hailey would fare, but most likely it would be tough going. And then, on the other hand, she could keep her mouth shut about what she knew - possibly to shelve it for a future publication - and work with this fellow. If he didn't come through, she could always back track. And if he did… Well, wouldn't that be fascinating!"

Apparently time was up. Nancy's window of opportunity was closing. Mr. Ogilvie was making his preparations to leave.

"So. You have to make a choice," Mr. Ogilvie said, as he began to fade.

"There is a choice?" Nancy asked.

"That's my girl!" Mr. Ogilvie said as he took her hand and shook it.

Nancy was left setting in her booth with one hand outstretched over her empty plate and wondering about whether she was making the best choice. But, it's not like she had an advisor.

A farmer, just down the way, was giving her odd looks. But Leland, sitting with Stan, figured they were up next and braced himself.

Leland and Stan

While Nancy appeared to be sitting in the corner booth conducting a conversation with her thoughts, Leland and Stan sat at a nearby table - some distance from the other patrons - having lunch.

"How do you think it will go?" Stan asked.

"Don't know." Leland shook his head. "She's real stubborn. Kids that age think they are invulnerable. And she's hooked into a hellofa story."

When Carmella appeared there was an uncomfortable confrontation.

"You go out with breakfast and don't return," she said as she set the menus.

"Yeah. I kinda got distracted." Stan smiled.

"You got a loose front tooth." Carmella pointed.

Stan indicated Leland. "Your tax dollars at work."

"Thanks," Carmella said to Leland, then set a water for Leland - none for Stan - dropped some menus and walked away.

Stan shrugged.

"How's it feel to be a father?" Leland cocked his head towards a disappearing Carmella.

"I don't know," Stan looked puzzled. "Must have had that portion of my brain cut out." He lit up a smoke. "The initial part wasn't bad though." He exhaled with a slight smile.

"You can't smoke in a restaurant anymore," Leland said.

"You're the Sheriff," Stan pointed out.

"The rules are the same for me."

Stan glanced around. "Let's see if anyone complains." He smiled.

"You're making me look bad."

"How so?"

"You're making me look either ineffective or partial. Take your pick." Leland noted the others watching.

Stan took another deep draught. "I pick …partial." He smiled. He ground out the smoke in Leland's coffee saucer while smiling at the other patrons. "It's my last bit of freedom, you know?"

Leland nodded. "I know."

"Makes a guy kind of rambunctious." Stan clicked all five fingers at once.

It was an interesting trick, thought Leland.

Stan did it with the other hand, when he saw it amused Leland. "Kind of like playing the castanets."

Nancy was obviously wrapping up business just a few tables away.

"Hope you don't mind. Habits like this keep me from killing people." Stan was putting on quite a show.

"I don't mind," Leland said. 'This guy is getting nervous,' Leland thought, and he couldn't blame him. He was more or less committing himself to life in the slammer. He must have that figured. "But you're attracting some attention." Leland indicated some interested patrons.

"I figure I could get outta here no problem and be on the loose forever," Stan declared, like a hopped up kid. "Those guys they got hunting me are real snails from my new, post-operated on point of view." He chuckled. "But to do that, I'd have to keep killing them. Them and other people - which doesn't bother me, except that *that* bothers me." Stan lit up another smoke. Leland said nothing. "I used to be a pretty good soldier, you know?"

"So I heard."

Stan nodded.

"Agent Hailey dug up your file, once we'd recovered your prints. You had several commendations, one for bravery," Leland spoke softly.

Stan nodded.

"Do you know that you are crying," Leland said.

"Shit!" Stan laughed through his tears, completely bewildered. "I was wondering where all this water was coming from on the table!"

Stan put his head in his hands.

Leland offered him his napkin.

Then Ogilvie appeared, surprising everyone as was usual. "Good day," he said. "Am I interrupting something?"

"Do you just drift around?" Leland waved his hand in the air, as if to drive away smoke. "Or do you actually stay at a motel somewhere around here?" Leland asked.

"A little of both actually. Hi Stan."

Stan looked up.

"I'm your Control," Ogilvie introduced himself. "It's time to come in."

"You know, I thought I'd talk to you about that." Stan took a long drag of his cigarette.

"That's a nasty habit." Ogilvie waved him away. He offered a coffee saucer where Stan could crush his cigarette out, and indicated he'd be pleased if Stan were to turn away to do it.

"Is it?" Stan blew smoke at him.

Little flashes of lighting and electrical sparks lit up Ogilvie. One ear burst into flame, and Ogilvie started slapping at it. Leland lifted his cup of water to toss at the man.

"No!" Ogilvie exclaimed, before disappearing altogether.

Both Stan and Leland stood mystified.

"I'd guess my Controller doesn't like cigarette smoke," Stan suggested.

"I'd guess," Leland agreed.

"What... now?"

"I'd put that cigarette out, for good," Leland said.

"Guess so." Stan crushed the smoke out, placing the

saucer/ashtray on a far table, while Leland fanned the air. "We really scared him off!" Stan grinned. "I wonder how that works?"

"I have no idea." Leland sighed.

He guessed their best option was just to sit and wait.

"Until the air clears, right?" Stan suggested.

"Right," Leland agreed.

"Doesn't look like he much likes water much, either."

Leland nodded, setting the glass on a far table.

Ogilvie

'What a day,' Ogilvie grumbled, as he made his way back to his tractor trailer encampment out Route 203 and three miles up a lone dirt road. His ear was killing him. "Shit!" He slammed the steering wheel. The good news was that it was 'all in his mind'. Ogilvie squeezed his eyes from the pain. But the bad news was, his 'mind' hurt like hell.

When he got out he noticed the dirt bike donuts cut in the dirt near the trailer's door on which "Fuck You!" was sprayed in black paint. Scratches on the lock indicated they'd tried to pick it. 'Kill them all. Kill them ALL,' Ogilvie recited, as he pressed the tiny pinhead button which freed the false lock front to swivel out of the way. Then he pressed his sweating palm onto the clear screen beneath. A green bar of light passed back and forth beneath it. When the green bar had turned pink, Ogilvie moved his eyes close to the glass and stared in. He moved his eyes two seconds to the right and two seconds to the left. The screen flashed once, and the door swung open. Ogilvie stepped inside. All of the interior lights and equipment immediately booted up upon his entry. The door closed and sealed automatically with a hiss behind. Ogilvie lay back in the soft consol chair, breathed out slowly and collected his thoughts in the dim, electronic light. First, of course, was to file the report. They would expect something begun within one minute of the door shutting. Then, if nothing were forthcoming, there would be black ops all over this place within the hour. He'd best get to work.

Ogilvie swore for the umpteenth time and stole a moment to wipe some digital salve on his throbbing ear, before beginning his debrief. The stuff was supposed to assist in the re-patterning of his mind. The Lord knew how. But within about thirty minutes he could expect his mind to have the basic structure of its shriveled ear reconstructed. His body was a sort of 'mold', as it had been explained to him. The digital salve increased the mind/body connectivity.

Having your mind floating around was no piece of cake, Ogilvie grumbled, as he went through his formulaic debrief boot-up on the keypad - especially when you were being used as a kind of test pilot. He was always lurching into unforeseen glitches. These minds, when dislodged from their home flesh, were sticky as all hell. Two days ago, Ogilvie had passed too close to a stray dog and spent six hours scratching fleas and eating soggy garbage out of a trash can, before he was able - by virtue of a Herculean effort - to wrench his thoughts free. GaaawwwhhD!

Smoke would apparently short them out. Ogilvie updated them about that. God knows what that glass of water might have done. Ogilvie pictured himself lying in the Prius mentally dead as a cell phone in the bottom of a lemonade pitcher. His job had become very high risk.

But whatever it was they had given him, ironically, made his mind very slippery when it came to connecting with his *own* brain. In fact, the damn thing was forever falling out of alignment for one reason or another. The other day his mind had fallen down inside of his shirt, like a cigarette ash. A very strange moment that was! Talk about connecting with your lower chakras… His intestines, especially, had made him feel as if he were packing tins of beef with monotonous, pressing moments. He'd have to explore himself further sometime when the time allowed. Here he was, out here doing this in hopes of being the first to connect with a whole forest - umpteen square miles of living, breathing, self energizing computing power. The strategizing he would be able to undertake would completely befuddle any who contemplated directing him! And yet, what interested him just as much of late was feeling the thoughts of his own heart, as it beat.

The irony of that was something he kept to himself.

Last Meeting

Ogilvie had to try again.

Re-enter Ogilvie, take Two.

Stan and Sheriff Leland were sitting just as he'd left them. Excepting that Stan was no longer smoking. He appreciated that. Ogilvie nodded at Stan.

Stan winked in return.

Ogilvie frowned.

Leland reassured Ogilvie who stood beside the booth. "Don't worry. No smoking. No water on the table. I'm carrying a gun. But it's only because I'm a Sheriff, and I have to shoot Stan, here, if he decides at any moment that he isn't going to follow through with this." Leland indicated Stan.

"No worries," Stan said soberly. "I'm in."

"Why's that?" Ogilvie asked.

"We're buddies, right?" Stan raised his brows. "You're on my team." He smiled.

Ogilvie shook his head, while sitting down to join them. Carmella was off talking to a pair of young farmhands on the other side of the room. The cooks were yakking back and forth in Spanish. Two older farmers sat at the counter discussing milk prices. "You told him?"

Leland nodded.

Ogilvie nodded. "You know then that where you are going is to prison."

Stan nodded.

Ogilvie continued. "That the Sheriff and I have an agreement that whereas you will not be harmed; you will also spend a lifetime under lock and key."

Stan nodded.

"And that's satisfactory to you?" Ogilvie asked soberly.

"I've had better offers," Stan acknowledged. "At least they seemed so at the time." He locked eyes on Ogilvie. "But, yeah, I get it. I'm a surgically enhanced killer without feelings of remorse. I've a danger to innocent people. If I were back in with the grunts I wouldn't give a thought to putting a round through me, myself."

"This is amazing," Ogilvie remarked, scrutinizing Stan.

"What's so amazing?" Leland retorted. "You took a decorated soldier, the pride of his unit - and turned him into a killing machine, which you then loosed on his home population."

"Yes." Ogilvie nodded, amazed. "And then he stopped."

"So far so good." Stan nodded.

"We operated upon your brain. But I'm thinking that your *mind* must still be intact." Ogilvie examined his eyes.

"But I *am* getting kind of itchy," Stan continued. "Perhaps we could get this thing settled."

Ogilvie blinked and turned his attention to Leland.

"Okay," Leland said. "So how do we do this?"

They paid their bill and got ready to proceed.

"Just one question I have," Leland said before rising from the table. "Why don't you come as you are, instead of this ghostly specter you inhabit? I figure you must know by now that I'm not going to shoot you. Especially in a spot crowded as this."

"And how do I - that is, 'we' - know that you have the authority to do what you say you're going to do." This other question came from Stan.

"That's two questions," Ogilvie said.

"And we don't care," Leland said.

Ogilvie didn't seem to mind spending a little more time.

He pursed his lips. "Firstly," he said, "none of the customers in here are going to have any idea what I look like, or that I've been here. All they are going to remember is their Sheriff and his guest acting very peculiarly, to say the least." Ogilvie smiled. "And secondly, I'm sort of Beta testing this thing." He indicated his presence with a flourish.

Ogilvie continued when he saw their looks of incomprehension.

"What you're seeing here is *emerging technology*. There are few *knowns*." Ogilvie had indicated his aspect as if a woman displaying her make-up. "We don't know its vulnerabilities. We don't know its powers. We don't know how it will act within any environment except by trying it out. So. That's part of my job."

"Looks to be risky," Leland noted.

"You're right. If you would have thrown that glass of water on me the other day, I might very well have gone dead as a cell phone," Ogilvie remarked sourly.

"So why do you do it?" Leland asked.

"You're up to 3 or 4 questions."

Stan reached across to the other table they were passing, to retrieve a glass of water. "And we don't care," he mimicked Leland.

Ogilvie rolled his eyes. "Fine. I suppose we can talk all day."

Leland listened, while Stan drank the water.

"The organization I work for… actually, I should say 'within', because I haven't any idea of what my actions will amount to. Ordinarily, I get some orders. I carry them out. I file a report. Money appears in my bank account. In fact, the players are so cordoned off; things are on such a high level of need-to-know basis, that in my whole career I'm only spoken with two or three players."

"Two or three?" Leland asked.

"Yes. You'll begin to understand as you become more comfortable with the arrangement." Ogilvie nodded spritely.

"See," Stan hissed. "It's just a matter of becoming more comfortable *with the arrangement*."

" And this is as true of people making the decisions as it is of the people carrying them out." Ogilvie looked around as if they should both be amazed. "We're *very* tightly run." Still no reaction.

"What I'm *getting* to is, that I couldn't assure you of whether I have any authority to do what we're proposing - even if I wanted to.

Actually, which I do… But it doesn't make any difference. I couldn't tell you what my next orders will be, anymore than you can. Except to say, that this is how it's done. I'm a field operative. I'm expected to make decisions as I see fit." Ogilvie smiled his thin, chilling assessment of how this information struck them.

"So we're not really sure of anything," Stan said.

"We have to believe we know what we're doing," Ogilvie said. "That's how this business works," he assured Leland. "Our superiors anticipate our actions will be as we've been trained, so that what we do can be anticipated. And in this way, few instructions ever need be issued and the cloak of secrecy is maintained quite tightly." Ogilvie looked down as he lowered his voice. "And, as you have seen, in some cases this command structure tends to allow things to get out of hand."

"Okay. You've started to convince me." Leland frowned.

"So. Now to why I volunteered to do the Beta testing." Ogilvie smiled, as they neared the door. He opened it for them, then paused. "But can you guess?"

"You want the power, just as you've said before. You want to plop your mind onto a big piece of computing substrate, just like a fly on shit, and gambol about peeling back the secrets of the Universe," Stan declared. "Why don't these alpha types ever just want to get laid?" He entreated Leland. "It would calm the whole world down so much!"

"I don't want to go there with you, particularly," Leland said to Stan. "But I have a guess as to why you're doing the Beta Testing," he said to Ogilvie.

Ogilvie nodded.

"I think it's because that's the only way you can be in on what you're up to… Which is probably just as crazy as it sounds." Leland shook his head, as if to shake off something crazy.

"That's right!" Ogilvie stuck the door hard, but it made no sound. At that moment he looked positively pleased with Leland. "Nobody in the *whole organization* knows just exactly where they are or what they are up to, except *me* - because I know where they are *headed*. I am right there - metaphorically speaking - sitting on the headlights above the front bumper!"

"And, depending upon what you tell them - you call the shots," Leland observed.

"Bingo!" Ogilvie slapped the door jamb soundlessly, again. "I think that I am going to enjoy working with you."

Stan tried hitting the door too, but it made quite a big sound and heads turned, so he stopped. Then, he realized they were all standing in the doorway and stepped through. Leland followed.

"Are we all crazy?" Leland asked. But he could only ask it of himself, as he was standing alone looking up and down Main Street.

Stan was gone along with the apparition of Ogilvie. Leland had been given a number to call anytime he had a concern as to the well-being of Stan. Ogilvie said that if he called that number, he would hear from Stan within the next 24 hours. Leland supposed that would have to do. Then he wondered if he'd bother to call.

"Am *I* crazy?" He asked himself again, kneading the scrawled phone number between his thumb and forefinger. He flicked it into the street.

Then for the next five minutes he looked for it, till found.

Eventually Leland would be told to expect Kimmel County's first arrival of Experimental Refugees, and that "materials would be arriving in the mail as to their care and feeding". Leland exhaled slowly. 'Well, at least it's over,' he decided. "At least for now," he said to no one, as he walked further into the street to stare at his burnt out Sheriff's offices. It was warm out. The sun was low on the horizon. Suddenly he felt very tired and a little sleepy.

His next thought was to call Agent Hailey. He was sure that she needed to have a drink.

ABOUT THE AUTHOR
(1927 - 2012)

Eldon Cene died in Lompoc prison in 2012 after writing 31 unpublished novels. (The second to the last of which, *The Cognitive Web* - the second in a trilogy - is featured here.)

Eldon often said that incarceration was "the best thing that ever happened to me. I got three squares and all the privacy any man could afford. I could never actually kick being a criminal. I'd thought it was just my true nature, until I got in here and realized that all I *really* wanted to do was to write and make up shit. After that I was through stealing. But I was still incarcerated."

He is currently buried in a potter's graveyard just outside the prison walls. "It's the only way some of us are ever getting out of here," he remarked.

He was born Sheldon Garvey in Pine Rock, Texas. But adopted Eldon Cene as his pen name, "'cause it sounded better," he said, "and like any good second story man, I was (s)eldom seen". All rights are controlled by Magic Bean Books.

- Carl Nelson, Executor

www.ingramcontent.com/pod-product-compliance
Lightning Source LLC
Chambersburg PA
CBHW060824120626
46557CB00001B/360